TONIC *and* BALM

TONIC *and* BALM

A Novel

Stephanie Allen

Shade Mountain Press
Albany, New York

Shade Mountain Press
P.O. Box 11393
Albany, NY 12211
www.shademountainpress.com

Publisher's Cataloging-in-Publication data

Names: Allen, Stephanie, 1962–, author.
Title: Tonic and balm / Stephanie Allen.
Description: First trade paperback original edition. | Albany, NY : Shade Mountain
Press, 2019.
Identifiers: ISBN 978-0-9984634-3-8 | LCCN 2018955654.
Subjects: LCSH: Medicine shows—Fiction. | Pennsylvania—History—20th
century—Fiction. | Race relations—Fiction. | BISAC: FICTION / Literary

"Come On Up" first appeared as "Sympathy" in *Crab Orchard Review*, vol. 11, no. 2,
Summer/Fall 2006.

Printed in the United States of America by Spencer Printing

10 9 8 7 6 5 4 3 2 1

Book design by Robin Parks

Shade Mountain Press publishes literature by women authors, especially women from
marginalized groups (women of color, LGBTQ women, women from working-class
backgrounds, disabled women). We aim to make the literary landscape more diverse
and more truly representative of the nation's artistic voices.

Shade Mountain Press is a sponsored project of Fractured Atlas, a nonprofit arts
service organization. The work of Shade Mountain Press is made possible in part by
the New York State Council on the Arts with the support of Governor Andrew M.
Cuomo and the New York State Legislature.

For Kurt

PROGRAM

COME ON UP

Ephraim Travers

───────

AS EPHRAIM watches, the farmer lifts the hood of the old Ford motor truck and steam billows out, rising up into the black Pennsylvania sky. The engine emits a few hiccoughs and burps, noisier than a Tin Lizzie, and dies. The farmer draws thumb and index finger down hollow cheeks and spits a gob into the dirt road. It is the only sound, seemingly, in all the cornfields for miles around.

Ephraim was asleep in the back, lying in a pile of onions, when the man pulled over and shook him awake. He hadn't been dreaming. He didn't dream. Wasn't a dreamer, his older sister, Sophie, sometimes said, because she knew this about him somehow though he'd long since forgotten ever telling her such a thing. The way she said it, looking over at him from the table where she was pounding dough, was one of the hundred reasons why he ran off from her neat little house in Albany, New York. Only to get himself into a pickle here, as Sophie would have said, miles from home and not a wheel to carry him farther.

Well, he doesn't care. He'll find another ride. Right now, though, the man who offered his last lift bends over the hissing engine. A kerosene lamp perched on the fender casts a weak glow across him, showing a threadbare cap and a shirt full of patches, a wiry neck and hands, molasses-dark skin that seems to absorb the night. Ephraim looks off down the deserted road.

"Reckon we be here a while," the man says. Then, to Ephraim, as he rolls up his sleeves, "Fetch me that toolbox in back, boy."

"Yessir," Ephraim says.

Out behind the truck, there is a faint glow to the night sky, like from leftover daylight or far-off rain. In the truck's bed, Ephraim can see the rising mound of onions, the faint shape of the burlap sack he's slept on, but nothing like a toolbox. It must be buried under the onions. He'll have to dig it out. He rubs his hands together, glances off down the road again, and this time sees it.

The glow isn't from rain. It is being cast up into the sky from a field a mile away. As Ephraim strains to see its source, sound touches his ears. Voices, music, thinned and tossed around by the faint breeze but still recognizable. He drops his hands into his pockets and walks toward the glow.

He imagines a big farm, or maybe a mill. But when he gets closer, he can see that the light comes from torches arranged around several tents and an open-air stage down in a sloping field. There are dark shapes of people milling around and a larger crowd seated before the stage, all of them watching something Ephraim can't quite make out. He hears the tinkling of a piano, laughter rising now and again from the audience.

Closer, and he can see on the stage a man playing a banjo and his companion, a stout woman in a glittery dress who dances around him in a funny way that makes her keep bumping into him with her hips or bosoms, drawing laughter from the audience each time. After the woman chases the banjo player off the stage, two men, one big and one small, stride out in dark suits speckled like they've been splattered with whitewash. The little one climbs onto the shoulders of the big one, starts juggling balls and then appears to start dropping them, but the big man catches them and throws them back into the air, and soon there are so many balls flying between them that Ephraim loses count. Five? Seven? Ten? The little man teeters and falls off, drawing gasps from the audience, but he lands on his feet without losing a single ball.

Ephraim creeps closer and watches a while longer as the singing and dancing and clowning and stunts are taken up by a succession of people, coloreds and whites more mixed up together than he's ever seen. Across the top of the stage is hung a banner with ornate lettering at a jaunty angle that reads DOC BELL'S MIRACLES AND MIRTH MEDICINE SHOW.

After a while, tired and yawning, he turns his attention to the buggies, Tin Lizzies, trucks, wagons, and mule carts lining the roadway. He still needs a ride. If he can guess the right vehicle, he'll be carried on his way by some unsuspecting farmer heading home after the show. He walks along, looking for a truck or wagon to his liking. In the two months since he left Albany, he has stuck with rides that would have put Sophie at ease, Negro farmers, jolly or taciturn or straight-arrow men like the onion farmer he left down the road. All of them gave a twelve-year-old Negro boy a ride and a bite to eat without a thought. Now, though, there is no telling who he'll wind up with, what they'll say if they catch him.

Don't give any of that white riffraff a chance to get their hands on you, he can hear his sister saying in his head.

But Sophie isn't here. He finds a big truck with a cloth canopy and a bed full of crates and boxes and climbs in. In a few minutes he's made himself at home and fallen asleep.

WHAT WAKES him up is someone pulling on his foot. Ephraim opens his eyes to full daylight, a vast space yawning where the crates that hid him rest no longer and a ring of faces now stares at him. Roughnecks, he sees at once. Four or five of them. The kind of white men who huddled on vacant Albany lots early in the morning, waiting for trucks gathering up workers for the docks down along the Hudson, and hung around saloons at night.

"Well looky here," says one, a bald and grinning man muscular as a horse who sounds angry and amused at the same time. "We got us a stowaway!" He yanks Ephraim by the ankle until he's dragged him onto the truck gate, where they surround him. "What you doin' in there, boy? You stealin' from us?"

"No, sir," Ephraim says. "I was sleeping."

Another one, a skinny older man with faded red hair and sun-squinted eyes, says to Ephraim, "You stay put." Over his shoulder, he says to someone else, "Go get Conger."

Ephraim knows better than to look into any of their faces. If he keeps his mouth shut, they might let him go. Out past them he sees nothing but cornfields. It dawns on him that he must have picked one of the show's trucks to sleep in, and his bad choice has left him exactly where he was the night before.

In a few moments another man whom Ephraim guesses is Conger arrives and exchanges a few words with the others. He is short, dressed like a dandy in a plum-colored, high-waisted coat and a matching bowler.

"Anything missing?" he says to the men, though he stares at Ephraim.

One springs into the truck and looks around for a moment before saying no, there isn't. He jumps out again.

"You think you're joining the circus?" this Conger says to Ephraim, coming closer and talking fast. "Well this ain't a circus, boy, it's a medicine show. And Doc Bell's med show don't take on tyros, got it? Last pickaninny I had ran off on me after a week. And good riddance, too! You got anything you can do, boy? What can you do?"

What can he do? Ephraim has no idea what the man is talking about. "If you don't mind, sir, I'll just be on my way," he says.

He slides off the gate, drops to the ground, and walks right through them. Nobody touches him.

"Wait a minute," says Conger.

Ephraim stops.

"I've got a job for you." Conger waves the others off and then beckons matter-of-factly to Ephraim, as if they've already discussed and struck some kind of a deal. "Come on. It's so easy a monkey could do it, and the pay's as good as you'll get."

Ephraim looks out over the cornfields, which stretch unbroken as far as he can see. Off to his other side stands one of the sagging tents, which by daylight looks more like some bedsheets thrown over a clothesline. It can't hurt anything to do what the man wants for a while, long enough to get himself some dinner, maybe, and his bearings. His stomach growls. He can always light out later.

"Yessir," he says, turning and following Mr. Conger into the field.

THE JOB turns out to be pasting labels onto amber bottles of tonic. Mr. Conger sets him up in the back of an emptied truck with a mountain of the bottles, a stack of labels that say DOC BELL'S VIM-TANA HERBAL TONIC and a paste pot and brush. Ephraim carries on with it all morning, until curiosity gets the better of him and he pulls the cork from a bottle. The scent of booze that wafts from inside, familiar to him from his days of accompanying his sister on her charity visits to tenements, wrinkles his nose.

In the afternoon, when he gets bored, his eyes wander back to the stage. Erected in front of another small tent, it stands empty now, but the blue and red bunting draped along its front edge and the white pennants flapping atop its support poles give it a festive air. Flanking the stage are two enormous panels. On the panel to the right of the stage, a curly-haired mermaid playing a banjo gazes out at him, her long fishtail curved fetchingly behind her. On the left floats a buxom angel in a flowing gown who smilingly drips a sparkling drop from her finger into a bottle labeled DOC BELL'S. Two or three times, Ephraim believes the angel and the mermaid are moving, that the show never stops, but after a while he chalks this up to being light-headed from hunger and a little disconcerted by so many new people around him.

And what people they are. Many of the performers wandering the grounds are in plain shirts, trousers, and dresses now rather than their garish costumes, but he recognizes most of them from the night before just the same. The sad-faced Negro lady who swallowed a sword, still in one piece the morning after, walking around in circles like she lost something. The blonde-haired lady who did the pistol stunts has shed her buckskin dress for a yellow frock, but she walks with the same swagger of the hips. And the acrobats, the tall, lanky one and the little one, travel together by day as by night, though now they argue loudly with one another. While Ephraim's staring at them, something passes close to him that momentarily blots out the sun—a man tall as a man and a half, dressed in a suit assembled from American flags. People flounce around in bright neck scarves or whistle loud tunes or lie in the grass like they just fell out of the sky there. He counts almost twenty of these peculiar folk before he loses track and gives up. None of them pay him any mind. When he gets tired of watching them, he goes back to pasting labels again.

Around dusk, when he is hoping food might be forthcoming soon, Mr. Conger shows up again. "Forget about that," he says, waving Ephraim out of the truck. "Come down here. I got something else for you to do."

Should he go? Ephraim watches Mr. Conger's back recede and wonders. These people seem harmless enough, even silly with their strange airs. But if there is no food in the offing, maybe it is time to be on his way.

Mr. Conger turns around and stares at him for several moments before he says anything. Then he smiles and says, "This ain't like nothing they got back at home, boy. Guaranteed."

Ephraim is sure he's already seen most of what the show has to offer, but he follows anyway. If it isn't like home, it's fine with Ephraim. Back there, oftentimes, they would hear about some child falling down the stairs and breaking its neck, or read about some poor woman forced out of her home and driven insane, and his sister would sit in the parlor chair and rock and weep and moan. If he came near to ask if he could help her, she grabbed him and held him to her, rocking them and sharing her grief over someone neither of them knew, until she sensed he was simply waiting to be let go. Then she pushed him away from her with a snort of disgust. Other days, he might be in the parlor alone and lift the pictures Sophie kept of their dead parents, one by one, from the small table by the window. He might finger the silver frames, trying to remember these people who died only a few years after he was born, when Sophie, much older than he, had been sixteen. But he couldn't recall them. They were only faces to him. *Try, try to remember!* Sophie would implore. *Surely if you try, you can remember your own parents!* Once he heard her tell a member of one of her women's groups about his dismal failure. *I can scarcely believe,* she said, *my own brother could be so cold-hearted!*

Mr. Conger stops in front of one of the tents, which has a banner strung across the front of it reading SHEBA, QUEEN OF THE NILE. At a ticket stand in front of the entrance, an old woman eyes him sourly. Lightning bugs begin to wink around them, and from somewhere banjo notes sprinkle the air. Off a ways from where Ephraim stands with Mr. Conger, there are already groups of scraggly white people arriving, farmers in overalls, farm wives in cotton dresses and heavy shoes, clutches of children milling around them, all finding seats among the sea of benches that have been set out in front of the stage.

"Now here's what I want you to do," Mr. Conger says.

He is close to Ephraim now, and he seems different in the semi-darkness, friendlier somehow, as if he likes Ephraim. He lights a cigar and smiles.

"Now Gert there will sell some tickets, see, and send the first bunch of rubes in. Only they won't find anything, and they'll come out complaining. Gert's going to send you in to see about it. You go on in and just wait for a minute. Nothing else. Got that? Count to sixty. Then you come running out of there screaming and hollering like you just ran into the Ku Klux Klan. You hear me, boy? *You fly!* And you keep right on running like you ain't planning to stop till you get to California. You think you can do that?"

"Run out of that tent?" Ephraim says, trying to see what's inside. The flap is closed, though, and he can see nothing. Even the dim images on the banner are impossible to make out in the dying light.

"That's it!" Mr. Conger says, grinning. "And make plenty of noise!"

And with no further explanation, Mr. Conger leaves him standing there between Gert and the tent.

Though he's confused, Ephraim stays put. A small, quiet crowd gathers in front of the ticket stand, waiting to go in. A few people stare at him, but most chatter with their companions, paying little attention to anything else until Gert waves the first in line forward to buy tickets. Three men and two women meander into the tent.

Those waiting continue their murmuring and shushing of children. Music from the stage drifts over and fills the air. A minute passes, then two. The men and women spill back out of the tent.

"Ain't nobody in there!" says one of the men, angrily waving his ticket. He hitches up his overalls. "This ain't nothing but a cheat!"

"Yeah," says another. "Ain't nothing inside o' there! Gimme my money back!"

Ephraim wants to run. But Gert turns around and looks at him for the first time, and Mr. Conger's words take him over and he mutters and backs into the tent himself as if he will attend to the problem.

As soon as the flap falls over the entrance, the noise muffles and the air tastes heavy as dirt. He sucks in a breath and then breathes out more easily. It is too dark to see anything in the tent, and he has no intention of poking around inside, looking for this Sheba. Maybe the tent is empty. Maybe this Sheba is some kind of wax dummy Mr. Conger hid somewhere inside the tent. It must be some kind of a hoax. Ephraim feels a vague shame, the singeing heat of Sophie's disdain at him for getting mixed up in something so dishonest, and he resolves right there to carry through with it all just as Mr. Conger told him to. He squares his shoulders, parts the curtain, and rushes out again, screaming at the top of his lungs.

The people outside are too startled to move out of his way. He dashes on, feeling a little foolish, but hollering for all he's worth and bumping and jostling hips and shoulders in his crazy flight away from the tent. Then he clears the edge of the crowd and barrels on across the dark field, giving it a few more squawks and screams before he guesses he's far enough away to quit the whole charade.

He turns around, his chest heaving, his eyes watering a little, and watches the result. Already the crowd has swelled to twice the size it started at. Yells and cries go up as the people push forward, waving hands, some clutching dollar bills, over their heads.

Ephraim's breath eases. He gets it now. He, Ephraim, has just put on a show as good as anything happening on the torchlit stage. But he and Mr. Conger and the old lady are the only ones who know it. He laughs out loud, then claps a hand over his mouth and looks around to see if anyone heard him. There's nobody there, though. He's fooled them all.

THEY LET him sleep in the same truck as the night before, which stays parked on the showgrounds when all the performers pile into cars at the end of the night. As he lies there, Ephraim hears them pass by, hooting and hollering and singing among themselves. He's asleep before the noise of them dies out.

And just that easily he falls in with Doc Bell's Miracles and Mirth Medicine Show. Mostly the performers pay him little mind as he slips among them, doing whatever chore Mr. Conger has given him, watching from the corner of his eye to discern their secrets. He gets to know the lady in the buckskin dress as Fannie Oakley, cowgirl and fancy shooter who loads her "pistols" with talcum power and topples her targets with a few well-placed threads. And Madame Svetlana, the medium, who starts her performance by reading the "fortunes" of one or two show members planted in the audience. Even the singers and dancers and comics have a jaded air about them and refer to the people who come to the show as "rubes" and "lot lice." Sometimes, when someone catches him watching, Ephraim gets a wink and a smile.

After a few days, Mr. Conger tells him Gert, the old lady, is sick, and he wants Ephraim to sell tickets to see Sheba, Queen of the Nile, that night. When Ephraim protests that he can't do it, Mr. Conger pats him on the back and says, "Don't worry, I'll show you how." He gives Ephraim some quick pointers, hands him a roll of tickets and a pocketful of change, and strides off. For what seems like hours, Ephraim is too stunned to move or speak. But then the shadows start to lengthen around him, and the sun fades, and before he knows it, he finds himself on the ticket stand with a crowd billowing around him. There's no need for him to say anything. The crowd is so anxious and restless he can tell that word of Sheba, Queen of the Nile, has gotten around. They pay him no mind until he yells that he has tickets for sale. Surprised white faces turn to him, and he braces for trouble. But after he fumbles through the first sales, people file in quickly. He almost overcrowds the tent before he remembers what Mr. Conger told him and makes everyone else wait.

By the end of the evening, after the last spectator has left Sheba's tent, Ephraim is exhausted. But nothing has gone wrong. And the next night, Ephraim sells tickets again without a hitch. The night after that, Mr. Conger shows him how to count out the wrong change. He explains it when he makes Ephraim the regular ticket seller for Sheba, Queen of the Nile, since he needs Gert elsewhere. It's all a matter of saying a few things to distract people so they won't pay attention to how much money he's handing them. Like how somebody's child is the most beautiful little baby he ever saw, and she looks just like her mama. Or how lucky someone is to be getting in to see Sheba before the crowd comes through and makes a big mess of everything in the tent. By the time people figure out he shorted them, the line will have moved on. He looks at Mr. Conger skeptically, doubting anyone will miss what he's up to.

But it works, just as Mr. Conger says. Pushing and shoving, their eyes bulging, their mouths full of shouts and gripes and such when they aren't the absolute first to get in, every rube on the lot Ephraim tries it on falls for it.

Late one night when the show's wrapped up for the evening and Ephraim believes all the performers have left for their boardinghouses, he sits on the gate of his truck, tired beyond belief. It's been a week now. Mr. Conger has told him he's welcome to travel with the show when they move on. No money for pay, of course, just a spot to sleep and food; nobody in his right mind pays good money to a pickaninny, he says, but Ephraim's welcome to tag along. And maybe he will. Perhaps he just will. His sister will be worried sick about him by now, but there's not much he can do for Sophie. He's never been a comfort to her, like her lady friends. He's sorry for it, but he's tired of trying.

A FEW DAYS later, Mr. Conger pulls Ephraim aside and says, "I have a new job for you."

"Yessir," Ephraim says, and drops what he's doing at once.

"Attaboy," Mr. Conger says, but he doesn't smile this time. "After tonight's show, I want you to walk Sheba back to her car. It'll be waiting up there."

Ephraim gapes at him. "She's real?" he stammers, watching Mr. Conger all the while for a sign his leg is being pulled.

But Mr. Conger is all business. "She ain't in the best shape," he says, lighting a cigar and puffing as if he never heard Ephraim's question. "Take it easy with her."

Through the afternoon, as Ephraim takes care of the chores he's been assigned, he ponders this new turn of events. If Sheba is real, how is it he hasn't seen her by now? And why doesn't she ride with the rest of the performers, anyway? He finishes cleaning mud off truck tires late in the day and takes his place outside Sheba's tent. For the first time, he looks carefully at the banners strung overhead. STRANGER THAN THE HOTTENTOT VENUS it says under one blurry picture—whatever that means. Under another, VERIFIED BY THE BRITISH MEDICAL SOCIETY. None of it tells him much about this Sheba. If he wants to know more, he'll have to go have a look for himself.

He steps in and lets the tent flap fall shut behind him. It's at least ten or fifteen minutes until full dusk, so he has time. It's stuffy and dark inside, just as he remembers, but now there is faint light in the far corner. As his eyes adjust, he sees the outlines of crates and boxes strewn across the floor. And he hears what he did not hear the first time he entered the tent: a heavy, rasping breathing that comes from the same corner as the light.

He moves forward cautiously, his ears pricked. This is not what he expected.

"Hello?" he calls out. "Anybody in here?"

Nothing comes back to him but the breathing, which gets louder and rougher as he approaches the dim corner.

The hair stands up on his arms a little. He's seen the faces of people coming out of the tent for many nights now, and he took most of them for foolish dupes tricked by his theatrics or Mr. Conger's shenanigans. Now he frowns. The breathing cannot be coming from Gert, who smokes and coughs but does not sound like the sound he hears. There is someone else in the tent with him.

The next moment he reaches a canvas inner wall of the tent, the shade that's been dimming the light, and steps around it. And he sees. But he doesn't know what he's seeing. A molten mass of shadows running together in an impossible way. He blinks, trying to comprehend what the kerosene lamp sputtering on the floor is showing him.

In front of him sits a Negro woman in a red dress. Baubles and beads decorate her bodice and sleeves. She rests slender hands and wrists on the chair's arms, sits motionless except for a slight trembling of darkness where her head should be.

Ephraim steps closer, staring still. And finally he sees that the shadows *are* her head—huge and swollen, floating as if without attachment above her narrow shoulders. It is splotched with patches of hair and glistens where the scalp stands exposed.

Sophie, at that moment, rises up in him. *Poor woman, poor soul, to suffer such a terrible affliction!* Weeping, wailing, Sophie is inside him, thrashing, writhing in an agony of mercy that starts to knot up every organ inside his body from his throat down to his bowels. *God have mercy on this poor, tormented soul!* But the woman raises her tremendous head and fixes him with a gaze that is as still and steady as the ground itself. Her eyes flick down his length, rise back to his face, and stay there.

Ephraim shudders. Shakes himself. Clenches his fists and bears down until Sophie and all her churning and torment are gone, expelled through his pores. He takes a deep breath, a full, fresh breath that feels good even in the stuffy air inside the tent. He steps forward and sticks out his hand.

"Evening, Miss Sheba, ma'am," he says. "Pleased to meet you. You can call me Ephraim."

ANTOINETTE IS her name, she tells him, as he escorts her later to the car. Her voice sounds like dried leaves blowing across a sidewalk. "Not Sheba."

"Yes, Miss Antoinette," he says.

With her arm in his, he walks her across the black field that cloaks the two of them in total darkness. Even the ground is invisible. He would like to laugh, laugh with her about this "Sheba, Queen of the Nile" game they play together, but he does not believe she would welcome it. She wears a hat now, an enormous black hat decorated with curls of ribbon and ornate bits of mesh, and though he cannot see it in the dark, he can feel it lifting and waving gently as she walks, like some great, silent bird hovering over them. She walks slowly, with the aid of a cane, forcing him to slow down until they fall into step.

He tells her about his first night, the screaming bolt he made from the tent, watching the results of his performance from afar.

"Were you hiding in there?" he asks her.

She doesn't answer him. There's only the deep silence of the Pennsylvania night, dragged back and forth by the rough sound of her labored breathing.

Well, she must be tired, he guesses. A whole night of playacting, and her health isn't good. But her grip on his arm is so firm it burns.

So he talks for a bit, rambling on about this or that, until he feels himself babbling. He shuts up. They've nearly reached the area where the show's vehicles are parked and others are loading equipment and piling into the cars that will carry them to boardinghouse rooms for the night. In a few moments, they are there.

14

The car she directs him to is a big touring model, already idling. He opens the door and helps Miss Antoinette settle herself in the backseat. When he hears she has stopped moving, he slams the door shut, and the car burps and pulls away, leaving him standing there alone. But he's not alone, really. The feeling of her, the impression, lingers on his empty arm.

He decides right there. Yes, he'll go. He'll stick with the show as long as they'll keep him on.

THE NEXT MORNING Mr. Conger wakes him early and sends him out to the boardinghouse where she's staying to run errands for her, get her anything she needs. "Then get your behind back out here," Mr. Conger says.

It's not far, the walk through hayfields and past red barns and lowing herds of black-and-white cows. The few farmers out working their fields ignore him. In no time, he's at the house Mr. Conger described, a dingy white clapboard with a rear porch tacked onto the second floor in back.

At the back door, a skinny Negro woman in a yellow headscarf gives him a plate covered in a napkin to take up since he's headed that way anyway. He mounts the outside stairs and finds the door he's been directed to. When he knocks, there's no answer.

"Go on in," says a voice from below. The woman in the headscarf, Ephraim sees when he peers over the railing, wiping her nose on her sleeve. "She don't never answer."

Then she's gone, and he wonders whether he ought to barge in. What else can he do? He pushes the door gently and announces himself as soon as he has a crack big enough to stick his face in.

Inside, the curtains on the window are drawn and the room lies in shadows. It takes Ephraim a minute to make out a high bed, a low bureau, and finally a chair beside the window, where she sits.

"Good morning, Miss Antoinette," he says. "I carried your breakfast up."

She is clad in a simple cotton dress now, faded and flowered, and in place of the elegant hat wears a soft turban that looks gray in the half-light. Her eyes, in the daylight, are the same inky dark as they were at night. Her spindly hands reach out for the plate, and he gives it to her. She removes the napkin and begins eating with her fingers without saying a word.

"She didn't give you a fork?" Ephraim says. "I'll go get you one."

And he leaves and runs down the stairs, startling the woman in the kitchen with his demand. He's back in a flash. Miss Antoinette takes the fork, glances at him, and then begins to eat with it. Her head looks larger wrapped in cloth than it did bare. He would like to touch it, not in the groping way the spectators in the tent want to, but to know about it. She is like nobody he has ever met before.

She hands him the plate, half-full of greasy food still, when she is done, and he takes it downstairs. Then he comes back.

"Mr. Conger said I'm to fetch whatever you need," he says.

She simply stares at him for a few moments, then shifts her gaze elsewhere. The moment she does, he feels cooler, more loosely assembled from fingerbones to knees to neck, and he wishes she would fasten her eyes on him again. *Look at me, Miss Antoinette*, he thinks, but he knows she won't and that it would be rude to ask. *What are you thinking about?* also rises to his lips, but he keeps that to himself for the same reason. It is hard to figure her, she speaks so little, and yet he cannot say that he dislikes it. He walks backward and settles himself on the bed, facing her.

Then she does look at him again, for a few moments, and he takes this to mean he should stay with her. So he does. Perhaps she will send him down the road, into town, to fetch her some headache powders like those Sophie kept in the bathroom cabinet. Or perhaps she will want him to escort her on a stroll out of doors to take in a little fresh air in her free hours. Maybe she will have him fix a shoe whose sole has come loose, or mend a tear in the seam of her frock. Read the newspaper to her. Sing her a song. Whatever she asks, he will do.

She asks nothing, though. He begins to fidget, wondering if he did something to displease her. He stares at her, ready to snatch his eyes away if she catches him. But after a while he relaxes, still watching her. And a while after that, he feels his breathing synchronize with hers, which is slower now, and quieter. And then stranger things happen. He falls into a stillness that erases all his thoughts, moving inward from the little worries that surround him to all his guilt about Sophie and home to that part of him that sits watching Miss Antoinette; and even that part of his thoughts he yields, and they slip away. His heart stops. He's sure of it. And it doesn't scare him. He only marvels, wishing he could raise a hand to his chest and feel the silence there.

When Miss Antoinette stirs, Ephraim cannot say how much time has passed since he entered her room. Minutes? Hours? Weeks?

"Go," she says.

That's it. No *Goodbye, Ephraim*. No *Good day to you*, or anything like it. He doesn't mind. He gathers himself and slides off the bed, not sure he remembers where the floor is going to meet his feet. But when he stands up, he is steadier than he was when he came in.

And he's steady when the sun, slanting bright at him, hits his eyes on the other side of her door.

THAT EVENING he looks out on the crowd forming to go into Miss Antoinette's tent and knows what he will do.

"Step right up, ladies and gentlemen," he says. Mr. Conger has not asked him to say any of this, but he knows Mr. Conger would be pleased to hear him. "Step right up. It's only two bits to see her, ladies and gentlemen. Sheba, Queen of the Nile!"

People stop talking among themselves and start looking up at him, as if they are surprised he can talk at all. Heads turn his way. He takes them in without the least flutter of nerves.

"You never saw anybody like her, ladies and gentlemen. I guarantee it. You never saw anybody like Sheba, Queen of the Nile, and it only takes two bits to go in there, ladies and gentlemen. That's all. You're gonna want to tell everybody you know you saw Sheba, Queen of the Nile."

He sells his first admissions much earlier than usual, well before there's even much of a crowd over at the stage. And he doesn't stop talking.

"Come on up, come on up here and buy your tickets," he says, and more come to him, wide-eyed and grinning.

"That's right, come on up here to see Miss Antoinette—"

He catches himself too late, tries to fix the mistake by just talking over himself.

"—see Sheba, Queen of the Nile, right here in her own tent, ladies and gentlemen. You're gonna be so shocked and surprised you might faint. Don't miss her!"

Nobody even notices his mistake. They keep coming.

A lot come. More than he's seen the last few nights. Ephraim keeps talking, except for a moment when he looks up and sees Mr. Conger standing off in the distance, watching him. Ephraim goes back to work. When he looks up again a few minutes later, Mr. Conger, apparently satisfied, is gone.

FOR THE NEXT few days things continue the same way, Ephraim bringing Miss Antoinette her breakfast, staying with her to await orders she never gives him, doing whatever work Mr. Conger assigns him on the showgrounds, hawking tickets at night, and escorting Miss Antoinette to her car. Ephraim begins to wonder where they'll go next, what it will be like to travel with Doc Bell's show.

He's standing outside Miss Antoinette's tent, watching customers start to gather, when he hears a noise behind him, a crash from inside the tent. He jumps down, listens next to the flap, but hears nothing more. What was it? There are only a few people waiting to go in, so he decides to slip in himself and check to see that everything's all right.

Inside he calls, "Miss Antoinette? You okay?" She doesn't answer, and while he knows there is nothing odd about this—not for her, anyway—it makes him uneasy, and he walks in deeper, picking his way around all the props he now understands to be "souvenirs" of all of Queen Sheba's "travels" around the world.

When he reaches the cul-de-sac where she sits, a shock runs through him. She is slouched sideways in her chair, her body in its red dress crumpled, her enormous, bare head lolling back. He lifts the lamp and shines it in her face, but she doesn't react at all. Just stares vacantly off into space, her eyes half-shut and seemingly focused on nothing.

An impulse makes him take her hand. Though he's never touched her before now and has nothing to compare it to, the limp feel of her palm and fingers scares him. He backs up a few steps, puts down the lamp and runs.

Through the flap, across the field that separates the small sideshow tents from the main stage and audience. Behind the stage he searches for Mr. Conger, gets a tip he's out by the show's vehicles, and runs on. When he finally finds him, Mr. Conger is talking to men Ephraim doesn't recognize, and he seems unhappy to be interrupted.

"Lot worse?" he asks, chewing his cigar.

"Yessir. She's real sick," Ephraim replies, wishing Mr. Conger would hurry up.

"Course she's sick, boy. That water on the brain's going to kill her one of these days. You see something new tonight?"

"Yessir," he says.

He's backpedaled too far to be questioned further, so Mr. Conger tells the men he'll be back and follows Ephraim back across the darkening field to Miss Antoinette's tent.

He's about to follow Mr. Conger through the tent flap when Mr. Conger waves him off and says, "Stay put," and disappears.

Ephraim does as he's told, though he can barely stand still now. The crowd's grown larger, and some of them start to ask questions.

"What's going on in there?"

"When they gonna let us in?"

"Hey, boy, what's this all about, now?"

He waves them off, but they won't go away. He can hear nothing from inside the tent. Someone puts a hand on his shoulder.

"Hey, boy—"

He bats it off, whirls and shouts, "Ain't no show tonight! I said no show! Now get away from here!"

They fall back from him.

"It says—" someone begins.

"Go on!" Ephraim yells, his voice rising. "Get out of here!"

Muttering, grousing, the people begin to move away. Ephraim turns, and turns again, watching them go and willing them to go faster. He wants to punch right through the flap and go in and see what is happening, but he holds back. Finally, Mr. Conger comes back through the flap just after the last local has wandered off to watch the performances over on the stage.

Mr. Conger looks around at the empty field surrounding them now and chews his cigar. Then he stares at Ephraim.

"You some kind of doctor now?" he asks.

Ephraim doesn't understand. "I'm sorry, sir?" he asks.

Out of nowhere, Mr. Conger backhands him. His ear rings like a train whistle and pain blurs his sight.

"You do what I tell you," Mr. Conger says. "You hear? From now on, you're back to pasting labels. Nothing else."

Mr. Conger whistles to somebody as he walks away, and a figure approaches. He points back at the ticket stand. The figure comes closer, and Ephraim sees it is the old lady, Gert, back to her old job. Her face screwed into a squint of disgust, she spits in the grass and steps up on the stand, where she proceeds to ignore him.

Ephraim stands there for the longest time, half-aware of a few people drifting over again, of Gert starting to sell them admissions. From the stage drifts the singsong cadence of a reedy man's voice exhorting the audience to save themselves from the languor and pain that come of impure blood, but Ephraim hardly hears it. Miss Antoinette must be all right, he thinks, but what he saw tells him otherwise and his legs twitch, urging him to defy Mr. Conger and plunge into the tent. But he doubts he would get past Gert, and finally he moves away, out into the field, into the dark, where there is no Mr. Conger, no stage show, nothing but the warm stickiness of blood on his cheek.

THE NEXT MORNING, when Ephraim awakens, it is to yelling. Shouting so loud it shakes his bones, and the rumble of truck engines all around, including the truck whose bed he has slept in.

But why is the engine running? His truck is one that remains parked on the showgrounds night and day. He looks out to see the old red-haired roustabout beckoning to him, the same one who kept the others at bay when they discovered him hiding that first day. Before Ephraim can open his mouth to ask what is happening, the man disappears.

Ephraim crawls out and stands in the daylight. What he sees makes his head swim. The field is empty of its stage and tents and performers. There is only trampled grass, muddy spots, papers blowing about. Ephraim whips his head around. The first car is just pulling onto the road, and behind it cars and trucks are stirring to follow.

"Mr. Conger says you're to stay put," says the red-haired roustabout, reappearing now to swing his wiry frame up into the truck's cab in a single, brisk motion.

"Stay till when?" Ephraim asks.

The man shuts the door on him without answering, and Ephraim finally understands. He's being left behind. They're not taking him along.

The wind goes out of him. It's too soon, too soon for them to leave—but nobody ever told him the day, ever said exactly when Doc Bell's Miracles and Mirth show would once again take to the road. But they can't be leaving him! It has to be a mistake.

He whirls around, looking for the car he knows better than any other. It is near the front of the caravan, and even running full-out, Ephraim cannot reach it until it is well on its way down the dirt road. He runs along beside it, yelling to Miss Antoinette, whom he can see through the side window in her big black hat. She will want him to come. He knows it.

She stares ahead.

"Miss Antoinette!" he yells. "Wait for me! Let me in!"

She looks at him. Then she turns her eyes away from him, back to the road. She doesn't lean forward to tell the driver to stop, doesn't open the door so he might jump in. The car begins to pull away from him, and all he can see is the dark cloud of her hat through the back window of the car.

He falls in the dirt, scrambles up, and chases the car again, yelling and screaming in a way that tears at his throat. He falls back from her car, and white and Negro faces alike watch him from the windows of other vehicles, grinning and laughing at him. He stumbles and falls again, but this time he doesn't get up as the caravan rumbles past him, one by one, until there is nothing but a quiet Pennsylvania day around him, just a few disturbed grasshoppers and his pounding heart to remind him there was ever anything else there at all.

SATURDAY EVENING, and the ladies of Sophie's Negro Women's League chapter gather slowly in her little parlor, each of them an assemblage of linens and poplins so fresh they still smell of the iron. Ephraim goes to the door each time there is another knock, greets the newcomer, lets himself be clucked over, takes hats, leads the way to where Sophie's guests sit in a circle, near the dormant hearth.

A month, now, he has been back, and when he glances at his sister, no longer does he see in her wide brown eyes the wondering about how long he will stay. He goes into the kitchen, pours hot water from the kettle simmering on the stove, and carries the teapot, teacups, sugar, cream, and spoons out into the parlor on a tray patterned with roses. Since he has been back, he has arisen every day at dawn, completed the chores Sophie set out for him, scratched out answers to the multiplication problems his sister has prepared for him so that he can catch up on his lessons before school begins in the fall. He passes a teacup to Miss DuBois, a plump lady with copper hair. He has accompanied Sophie to the crowded homes of the poor, where she delivers impassioned lectures on the benefits of scientific childrearing. He has stood with his sister on a street corner, Sophie damp from a light morning rain but refusing to go indoors, and watched a group of Negro troops back from the Great War walk silently down Calders Avenue. They carried white banners hand-lettered in red with messages saying things like UPHOLD LIBERTY FOR ALL and STOP THE CRIME OF LYNCHING.

This afternoon, the women of Sophie's chapter of the Negro Women's League have gathered to parse and package donations from their church to send to the families of dead Negro soldiers. Rags and castoffs, it looks like to Ephraim. Junk he would be embarrassed to give to anyone. Dolls with cracks, clean but threadbare bloomers, bent forks and hatpins, tiny thimbles. The ladies make neat bundles, bind them in twine, and then commence to writing long letters full of ink blotches to accompany each parcel. These take the longest time, and they converse quietly as they write.

Sophie looks up from her letter and sees him hanging back at the edge of the room. She's a little plumper now than she was when he left, and Ephraim wonders if she has had to let out the plain, slate-gray frocks she customarily wears.

"Put away the tea, Brother," she says in her soft but firm voice. "Come and join us."

Reluctantly, he puts the tray on a table. Sophie pats the seat of an empty chair beside her, and Ephraim slowly sits down.

He started to tell Sophie about Miss Antoinette once. His sister's eyes brimmed with tears. When Ephraim saw this, he stopped, never even getting to the part about how Miss Antoinette left him behind. Left to itself, his hurt and confusion withdrew to a place deep inside him and settled among his stomach and liver like a new organ that throbbed quietly throughout the day. He has not said a word about the rest, the roustabouts, the performers, the playacting, the phony medicine. And as if she doesn't really want to know, Sophie hasn't asked. Ephraim has been waiting patiently for Sophie and the tasks she sets for him and the instructions she gives him for being good, for helping the unfortunate, for giving himself to the Lord's service, to blot all of it from his memory. He has tried to put his faith in doing exactly what Sophie asks.

She hands him a lumpy parcel and a clean sheet of paper. She merely nods at the inkwell and pen lying on the small table between them and fixes him with her deep brown eyes until he takes the pen in hand. Using the parcel as backing, Ephraim spreads the paper. He has no idea what to say to people he's never met, never even seen. He wants to get out of the stuffy room, away from this thing Sophie wants him to do. But he stays.

"To the family of Bliss Thompson," Sophie says. "Shall I spell it for you?"

Ephraim shakes his head. *Dear Family of Blis Tomsun,* he writes slowly and awkwardly. Then he bites his lip, thinking of what to say next. His parents, those grainy faces in Sophie's photographs, would surely be pleased to see him now, learning the ways of Sophie's boundless kindness. What does it matter what someone in a trifling traveling show would think of him? But he is speechless, he is not trying hard enough, he is failing Sophie again.

Sophie grasps his shoulder. "Brother," she says, "this is not the time to daydream. Keep to your task."

The throbbing in him dulls to a buzzing, like a fly trapped in his chest, one he can ignore. He puts nib to paper, and the rest comes to him easily, as if he knew it all along. *The trials of this world are only the means by which we become stronger. God sends us no trial too great for us to bare. From today's misforchen springs tomorrow's firm resolve.* He dips his pen and continues. *We are all marching toward a greater glory. There is peace in knowing that we have done our best to serve others. Time heals all woonds. Tomorrow is another day.*

Sophie smiles at him, and Ephraim continues. *To seek after things we can never have is to find only sorrow.* He dips his pen and writes, and the words become his own.

A BUCKET OF BEER

Louise "Ma" Fleet

———

BOY'S GONNA be the ruin of us all. I keep telling Fleet a boy that dumb ain't nothing but trouble, but he don't want to hear it. When it come to bad news, old man's got a way of keeping out of earshot. Problem is, that don't make it go away.

"Haines!" I yell at the boy. "Get your keister over here!"

It's a Monday afternoon, hotter than perdition, and Doc Bell got the show set up in a little meadow between a melon patch and a muddy cow pasture. Haines across the way trying to sweetheart that Marie gal. Getting all up next to her, throwing off those little strokes on his guitar like it's gonna get him somewhere. Fool the only one in Doc Bell's med show who ain't figured out she don't care for folks of the male persuasion, and she encouraging him by grinning and fetching like she love nothing better than getting in menfolk's pants.

"Haines," I holler, "boy, I mean now!"

Fleet, sitting there next to me with his banjo across his lap, just smile like it's all some kinda big joke, getting this knothead to listen to me. "My apprentice" is what he been calling the boy, as if putting on airs gonna make it all better. Here we are, him in his twilight years, the two of us towing God's own fool all the way from Florida up to Ohio. And what for? Just to add a little guitar to our bits that we ain't needed for the last twenty-some-odd years. Till now. Now my husband got it in his head we need this pickaninny fool so fresh off the farm he still got straw between his teeth.

"Lay off, gal," Fleet say. "Let a young man have some fun."

Sometimes I wonder why I married the man. I might as well be talking to a mule, stubborn as he is. Every new gray whisker he get only seem to make him worse. It's him and Doc Bell's right-hand man, Felix Conger, that cooked up this Haines idea. And it's him and Conger who ain't gotten nowhere teaching the boy the simplest bits. "Beans and Porridge" he can't do 'cause he trip over the lines, the ones he remember. "Gilhenny's Ghost" he can't do no better though the ghost don't speak ten words altogether. "Knot in the Wood" just about had him in tears though I seen ten-year-old boys could pull it off just fine. Can't sing. Can't dance. Can't even do a decent fall on his keister except when he ain't supposed to, and then it seem like the ground made of metal and his butt is a magnet. All he want to do is play that damned guitar, as if people gonna line up and sit there just to listen and watch him move his hands.

"Haines! Don't make me come over there and get you!"

Fleet just sigh and cross his legs and give off one of them "I can't do nothing with the gal" looks of his. Running his knobby fingers over his banjo strings like he don't know me. Sitting there in a chair in the middle of a field with everybody running around to get Doc Bell's show ready for tonight, checking props, hauling crates of tonic and salve, setting out benches, limbering up for their bits. When I stand up and look down at that grizzled head of his, I can almost believe he's well nigh sixty years old. Sixty years. Look gaunt as a old, gray scarecrow hung up by his suspenders these days, all sunk around the eyes, and think I don't notice it, but I do. And I wonder what it's like to be so far down the road of life. If he feel some kind of cold in his gut in the morning, if he think twice at night about closing his eyes. If this Haines boy is something he feel he gotta have before it's too late to have it.

I leave the old man there. Haines and Marie setting out on the edge of the stage, don't see me come up next to them, they so busy talking. Boy's well-fed, I gotta give him that, big and strapping as he's weak in the head. And I bet that pecan-brown face and sappy grin of his get him plenty of female attention. Enough to fool him into thinking ain't a gal in bloomers won't fall all over him. Just when I think I seen it all, the nitwit actually take Marie by the hand.

"Just use the side of your thumb," he say. "That's it."

And he bring her hand down across the strings of his guitar to make a chord. Of course she start giggling like a natural idiot. I look at Doc Bell's painted angel and his mermaid floating over us and I almost feel sorry they gotta listen to this mess.

"You doing fine. Now put your hand here."

He wrap her fingers around the neck of the guitar and push a couple of them down on the strings. Then he bring her thumb down again. And that don't sound half-bad neither.

"That's all I'm doing. Ain't nothing more to it."

She giggle some more, and they do it all over again.

I'm about to snatch the guitar when he ease it out of her hands and start playing it hisself, looking at her the whole time like they got some great secret between the two of them. He start off doing some slow, simple strumming, then he pick it up a notch while she watch his hands. And I see what he up to. Messing with her. Showing her a few simple chords, then whipping them off so fast she can barely see what he doing. He speed it up some more, then he make a little shift and slow down, and he's back to the chords he started from.

Haines don't see a thing around him no more, he so busy playing. But Marie look up at me and smooth her frilly yellow frock with her hands and bat them long eyelashes like she mean to blow out a candle.

"My land, Miss Louise!" she chirp. "Isn't he just *charming*?"

Charming? Right now I don't care if he stand on his head and get off a few verses of "Dixie" on a pair of spoons. I'm about to take him by the neck when he finally stop playing.

"You looking for me, Ma?" he ask me, grinning.

Ma and Pa Fleet's a stage name, I told him a hundred times—quit calling me that! Fleet ain't your father, and I ain't the mothering type. If I ever found out that fool was blood relation to me, I'd take a straight razor and open up every vein I got.

But I'm too tired to say it again. Tired all the time these days. Can't even remember what I wanted with the boy now that I got him in front of me. If this is what forty-five feel like, I gotta pay tribute to the old man for being on his feet at sixty at all.

THE SHOW GO off that night just as tired as I feel. We all do our bits best we can, but you can see the folks out there watching ready to nod off to sleep. Fannie and her trick guns and all her sashaying don't stop the yawning, and it look like Matilda gonna have to run herself through with a sword just to get a smile or two. I can tell by the look on Conger's face that he worried we ain't gonna be selling much of Doc Bell's cures at all.

Things perk up when Doc Bell come on and do his first lecture. He stride on out in his black frock coat and trousers, looking like a undertaker, all somber and grave. He tell this story about a sister of his he lost to piles, and how he dedicated his life to relieving the suffering of other poor souls in the viselike grip of this terrible condition. Every rube out there look skeptical at first, thinking to hisself that ain't nobody ever expired from piles, for Pete's sake, and that's just what Doc Bell want them to think. He just go on, talking about how his sister had her babies and then got to feeling just a little sore and itchy, then how the pains come on her every time she sat down to rest her body a little, and the rubes out there start to fidget on them hard benches whether they got piles theirselfs or not. Then Doc Bell really get started with the blood and screaming and fainting, and all them people out there get real quiet, not even looking at each other no more. By the time Doc Bell finish, he got piles sounding worse than cancer, and there's more than a few teary eyes when he lay his dear sister in her early grave with them little corn dolls her babies made to send their mama off to heaven with. Then he take out a little corn doll hisself and hold her in his big hands and get quiet, and don't nobody say a word. "Friends," he finally say, his head bowed down and his voice all broke up, "that's when I dedicated my life to this holy work, this healing profession, this queen among all the arts known to man. Tending the sick."

All of us in the backstage tent listening to him too, even though we heard this story a thousand times. First it was Doc Bell's cousin, then his brother, then his mother, with dyspepsia for a time, and later with liver troubles before he hit on piles. Few more years and his whole clan back in Indiana gonna be wiped out. Still, just listening to him, you want to reach in your pocket and buy a tin of Doc Bell's Septo-Soline Salve.

And people do—at first, anyway. But all our singing and dancing and comic bits and special acts that's supposed to plump them up for the second lecture just seem to wear them out. By the time Doc Bell come on again in his Indian headdress and buckskins, them rubes about the most hangdog lot you ever seen. He get them to buy some, but not much. And by the third lecture, you'd think the poor man was talking to the headstones in the local graveyard. Nobody move, nobody blink, and not more than a few souls buy a thing.

So Felix Conger round us up the next afternoon. Tonight's show supposed to be the last one we play in this godforsaken place, and we all so fidgety we can barely stand still.

"We're staying here another few days," Conger say, touching every one of us with his beady black eyes. "Doc Bell thinks this place's got potential we haven't even scraped yet."

Fleet just shake his head and *tsk-tsk* a bit, but other folks don't take it so calm as that. Fannie make like she gonna faint she so overcome with the news, and Matilda take it upon herself to spit in the grass. Conger give her a dirty look but don't say nothing to her. He just go on talking while one of the roustabouts, that bald fool with muscles for brains, keep right on laughing.

"And we're gonna make some more changes, too. Big ones!"

He fiddle around with the lineup, moving people up or down, switching bits and acts around. Then he say to the acrobats, "Carmoody and Pete, you two sit out the show tonight."

Everybody fall silent, even the roustabouts. Switching people around is one thing; we all know we gotta swallow that from time to time in this business. But getting put out of the show's a whole nother matter. Maybe it don't mean a thing, but maybe it mean Conger about to try to get rid of you, too. Carmoody, the big one, look at Pete, the little fella, and the both of them look like they want to cry.

"Now, ain't no call for that," Fleet say quiet next to me.

But Fleet don't want to look at the truth. And truth is, the problem ain't the tried and true med show bits people been happy to come out and see every year for long as Doc Bell been on the road. Some of Doc Bell's troupers saying it was setting out a week early in the spring that got us off to this bad year we been having. Others got the notion we picked up some kinda ill spirit when we detoured through that Indian graveyard in Turkey Notch, South Carolina. But most of us know what's the matter.

"I know what we ought to be dropping," I say.

Fleet shoot me a look and roll his eyes. "Gal, don't you start in on Haines again."

"Fine, then," I tell him. "You go right on thinking that dub ain't a millstone round all our necks. That water-head gal even worse."

We had a black cloud hanging over us ever since we took on the sick gal Doc Bell got parked in a tent for a freak show. I ain't one to question the man after all these golden years we had under his wing, but a thing like that in a med show bound to draw trouble.

Fleet turn hisself around. "You ought to be ashamed, Lou. Speaking ill of a poor, sick gal. And a *colored* gal at that." He pause like he been struck dumb by the very idea. "What's got into you lately?"

He rest a hand on my back and look at me all sad and concerned like he think my mind giving out on me. But I let it go for now. Stubborn as he is, he can't keep his head in the sand forever.

NEXT MORNING, Conger got us out early to work on our bits, yammering on and on so after a while I don't even hear him. I get to thinking about that home life I left behind. All that cooking and cleaning and ironing and tending to babies when the whole of Baltimore was out there waiting for me. My folks didn't never get no more than a few blocks away from home, and soon as they got the pork hocks or tarpaper or preaching they wanted, it was right back to those three little rooms they fixed up as nice as they could. My mama had a way with a needle, and she did up doilies and curtains and samplers till there wasn't one bare patch of wall or floor. And my daddy was handy, too, made us lazy Susans and footstools and shadowboxes and shoescrapes until you couldn't walk across a room without tripping over something. They was good people, but I wasn't the home kind like them. Soon as I was fifteen, old enough to go hear Lindy's Black and Tan Minstrels when they come to town, I was gone.

Ain't never been back, and got no wish to go now, so I tell myself there's worse things than putting up with Felix Conger prancing around in front of the stage in his suit and spats, barking orders that don't do nobody no good.

Haines fouling up his part as usual, no matter what we do. We give up on a few numbers that Conger want to try and settle on something simple, "Mabel Carey Gonna Marry." Fleet set up his banjo, run through the first few verses, then wait for Haines to come in like the other suitor saying his bit about Mabel. Only Haines don't open his mouth or pluck a string when the time come.

"I mess up?" Haines ask.

"Naw, not at all," I say. "You gotta do something before you can mess it up. You ain't even get that far."

Fleet explain to him again what he need to do, and Haines play the first verse of it. Then Fleet start at the top once more and this time Haines come in where he supposed to, but he play right through my part where Mabel come on.

"Hold it, fool!" I yell before he get too far.

Haines nearly drop his guitar.

"All right, stop right there," Conger say, jumping up on the stage.

I'm thinking this gotta be it. Nobody got the patience to do this forever. The boy ain't cut out for Doc Bell's show, it's plain to see, and no amount of head-knocking ever gonna get a whole routine through that thick skull of his, no matter how beautiful he play a guitar by hisself. And he do play beautiful. But you gotta do more than that to get by in the med show business. I seen a lot of performers come and go over the years, bad ones, good ones, everything in between. Them that last wasn't always quickest with a joke or lightest with a step. They just the ones that do whatever it take, no matter what. This boy Haines, he just ain't the med show kind.

Conger take out a cigar and chew on it. "Louise," he say to me, "go get yourself a drink of water."

At first I think I ain't heard him right. Mighty thoughtful for a slave driver. But he stand there waiting, so I hitch up my dress and climb off the stage and I tell Fleet to come on.

"Fleet's staying," Conger say.

I look at them, and I see it in their faces. They got something going they cutting me out of. Not a one of them look me in the eye.

"Go on, take a rest," Conger say out the side of his face.

And even though I'm mad enough to spit, I don't know who to be mad at. Conger always been a snake, and a snake he always gonna be. Fleet and I had rows enough and sure to have many more. But Haines, baby-faced and dumb as dirt, Haines? Haines got the jump on me?

"Hell with all you hyenas," I say.

"Now, Lou," Fleet say.

"Most *specially* you."

"Louise," Conger say, but I ain't having none of him, neither.

I just show them all my backside, like none of them's more than a trifle I just as soon forget.

WHATEVER THE three of them got bubbling on the stove, they don't bring it out for the show that night. Things go along in pretty much the same sad and sorry state they been stuck in for weeks in spite of all of Conger's shuffling and tweaking. Batch of Doc Bell's Columbium Compound go missing. A tent fall over for no good reason. Fannie come down with a case of laryngitis. And as if all that ain't enough to show that Lady Luck washed her hands of us, Kidwell sprain a ankle doing his Irish lush bit.

By the time they get him in the backstage tent, Kidwell look like a ghost. Conger send somebody off to get the boozer doctor, who come wobbling in looking about drunk enough to bust up Kidwell's other ankle. Me, I'd take Doc Bell and his swill in a pinch any day, but the German go to work and soon got Kidwell all in splints and wrapping. "Stay off it," he grunt, like Kidwell was fixing to get up and dance the polka.

The last morning of our extra week, I find my husband and Haines setting out in the yard behind the boardinghouse on bushel baskets. I ain't been sleeping well, and it's starting to catch up with me, but I ain't so worn out I don't notice they quit playing when they catch sight of me heading their way.

"Word going round is Doc Bell ain't gonna be paying this week," Fleet say, fooling with the pegs of his banjo while he speak.

"That so? Your apprentice put you wise to that?" I ask.

"Naw, gal, just going around."

"Well, it ain't no big surprise, old man. We got troubles enough to fill a ocean, and more is bound to follow them."

Fleet give me a funny look, like he thinking, *What more?* but then again he don't want to hear no more about it, neither.

I'm about to ask what's up when the sky start dripping on us. Haines jump up on his feet and grab a burlap sack off the ground.

"Shoot," he say, hitching up his pants and fumbling with his bag. But the bag come open 'cause he got it turned half upside down, and out fall all these shiny black phonograph records.

When I pick one up it's heavy as a couple of tin plates and just as cool. It got a black label with swirly silver letters going around in a circle. Haines bend over and scoop up the rest of them, but he think twice about taking the one I got out of my hands.

He and Fleet keep their mouths shut and look around all over the place, everywhere but at me.

"One of you gents been stashing a Victrola in your prop trunk, now?" I ask the two of them.

Fleet just bow his gray head and start strumming his banjo soft like he do when he mean to calm me down. That sweet stuff he so good at, kind that come wrapping its arms around you and kissing you up behind the ears. But I ain't having none of it today.

"No, ma'am," Haines say, all sheepish. He look over at Fleet. "But folks has them everywhere now, you know. They ain't hard to find no more. Many a house got one tucked up in a corner, even folks way out in the country where—"

Fleet shoot him a glance and he swallow what he was going to say. I look from one of them to the other, but now they both got their heads down like a matched set of guilty scamps.

"Well, nice to know you got so much money you spending it on what ain't no good to you most of the time," I say. "This what you two and Conger been up to when I ain't around?"

Haines look at Fleet and then back at me, wondering what to say. Fleet don't help him out.

"It ain't quite ready, yet, Ma," he finally say. "But we was playing this one."

And he take out one of the other records and hand it to me. It's "Ludie Bailey" by some outfit name of the Flat Street Jass Band, he tell me.

"Since when you need somebody to show you how to play 'Ludie Bailey,' old man?" I ask my husband. "We been doing it for twenty years."

Nobody say nothing.

I turn it over in my hands. "So what this Flat Street Jass Band sound like?" I ask.

Fleet's hand fall still, and for a moment don't neither of them make a sound. Then Haines start strumming. Fast. He run through something a couple of times before I recognize he even playing "Ludie Bailey," but fast and different, not like doing it ragtime but like he mean to tear the thing up in pieces. And while he whipping along on his guitar, Fleet start throwing some banjo licks in the mix. When I don't expect it, Fleet start singing.

Don't you tell me nothing, Mama,
I already got the news.
Don't you tell me nothing, Mama,
I already got the news.
Got me feeling something awful
From my head down to my shoes.

I want to throw up my hands and say, "Whoa!" but the way the notes flying, I lose track of all that and try to keep up instead. But Fleet launch into the next verse before I can get the reins, and Haines near to drowning him out he going at that guitar so hard.

> Take my hat and take my money,
> I don't need them anymore.
> Take my fiddle and my overcoat,
> Don't need them anymore.
> When your woman double-times you
> What's the use of all that for?

Then they fly into a break and Haines take over completely. Running up and down the strings, left and right, till I got no idea what he doing at all. Fleet tapping his foot, though, tensed up and looking for where he supposed to come in again, and I wonder what's he hearing that I don't.

Next thing I know, they done. Rain stopped, too. I ain't done a thing but listen, but I'm all out of wind just the same. Haines sit there twitching his knee like he can't wait to take off with another number, but he keep his head down like I might wallop him one if he do. But I ain't got no wallop left in me. Fleet look up at me out of them soft and rheumy brown eyes of his, eyes I know so well, every crease and every wrinkle around them, like it make him sad to finally show me what it is that been working its way between the two of us.

I give Haines back his record and walk away. Down the hill from the boardinghouse, to the little stream that run through a clump of brambles and blackberries so thick you can't see no water. You just hear it rushing on.

Been a long while since our best days, nobody need to tell me that. Back then, we rolled into a new town like a chariot bringing down a little slice of heaven. Seem like every night all the people that could put together four wheels and a donkey come out to see us, till all those smiling faces stretched out so far you lost them in the dark. Mamas with babies, menfolk with their hair parted and spit-combed, even old folks so feeble they gotta be carried out to the benches sometime. Every night for a week they come, and we make them forget they got pigs to slop and cabbage to hoe. And after Doc Bell's show wind down for the night, sometime, Fleet and me, we'd go off and play a gig in some colored folks' front room, pick up a little extra. And how I got the people going, with a shake and a shimmy and not much more. Some nights they was tired and vexed, pressed on all sides till they was about to bust and take some cracker by the neck, but they come hear us play instead. And by morning they ready to fall down and sleep. Just sleep like babies.

How I remember them days. Fleet and me, we didn't have no money, didn't have no sense half the time, played for next to nothing. Just played for the people, that was all.

BEFORE WE start the last show that night, Conger call us together and say he got a few things to announce. Carmoody and Pete up first today. That roustabout Lily hurt her wrist, so Haines of all people gonna be driving one of the cars when we shove off tonight. We all waiting to hear something about where we heading when we leave this blasted place, but Conger just tell us to get moving.

It ain't like me to lose track of the time, but dusk creep up on me and next thing I know, Fleet hustling me into the backstage tent. All Doc Bell's people in there, bumping against each other getting ready, running on or off the stage. I just sit over in the corner quiet till it's time for me and Fleet to go on.

Then, "Come on, gal!" Fleet saying, shaking me by the shoulder.

And we out there with a sea of faces looking up at us. Fleet start picking his banjo, and I step up and put my hands on my hips and sashay right out to the edge of the stage in my purple dress and open my mouth.

Don't give me no shotglass,
Don't hand me no cup,

I ain't here for dainty tea!
I got me a thirst that'd burn down a house,
It's a bucket of beer for me!

I turn around and smack my lips and throw Fleet a thirsty look, like I mean to wrap my legs around him tight enough to break him in half. He rock back on his heels and drop his banjo, then he pick it up and drop it again, and I can hear folks laughing at how scared to death of me he look before he start picking again.

I take a bottle of perfume out of my bosom and squirt myself round the neck with it and walk around behind Fleet with my eye on him while I sing the next verse:

Don't ask for my husband,
Don't bother the man,
He's out with his mule Annie Lee.
I got me a thirst that'd burn up a house,
It's a bucket of beer for me!

Fleet jump off his stool, clowning like I'm about to grab him, then he take his stool across the stage and sit down and start playing his banjo again, watching me like a mouse watching a cat all the while. Folks having a good laugh now, and I want to stay here forever, right here where me and Fleet fit together like there ain't more than a year between us and never will be. But when I turn myself around to sing the next verse, nothing come out of my mouth. Been singing "Bucket of Beer" for umpteen years now, and I go and forget the words. Just like that they go out of my head, and I stand there staring at the people like they gonna tell me what to do next. I want to grab on to them notes Fleet playing behind me, but I can't. I look back around at Fleet, but the look on his face say, *Gal, what you doing turning your back on the crowd!* I get a breath and turn back around quick.

Fleet step it up behind me, playing so loud and hard he almost drown out the whispering out in the audience. And I forget the whole damned skit. The people start up chattering like they sitting round the dinner table now, talking and pointing at me, and like a fool I just stand there. Ain't nothing Fleet can do, and I know it. And ain't no kind of cutting up gonna cover the trouble I got us in now it's gone so far, neither. And then, like I just got some joke, the words pop back in my head, and I sing.

> *Now don't get me wrong,*
> *He provide for me fine,*
> *When it come to the baubles and beads—*

Something plop me in the belly, and I look down and see a carrot laying at my feet.

> *Got fine, fancy shawls and velvet shoes, too,*
> *And all of the money I needs.*
> *But a gal like me with a six-plug drive*
> *Like to get up a little speed!*
> *I got me a thirst that'd burn up a house—*

Something wet smack me in the face. I look down, and a busted tomato sitting on my shoe, dripping seeds and goo. Fleet keep playing, but them people out there, they just stare at me, not laughing, not even smiling.

I know what I'm supposed to do. You gotta stick it out, hang on till you got them back with you again. But I turn around and walk off that stage. "Gal, where—" Fleet begin when I pass him by, but I don't stop. I go right on through the flap, into the backstage tent, down the stairs, which I got to think hard about to keep from falling down.

"Louise!" Conger say, and throw up his hands. "What the hell do you—"

But I don't stop for him, neither. I walk right through the middle of everybody staring at me and out the back of the tent, out in the dark and the air where there's nobody but me. I go under a tree and let it hold me up though I don't trust that it ain't gonna move. My head so light it could float right off, the rest of me want to sink into the ground, stars popping right in front of my eyes. Nothing like this ain't happened to me since back when I started out. It don't make no sense. I'm a little tired, but I been tired before. It don't make no sense.

Then my throat choke up and everything go all blurry. And just when I think I'm gonna fall on the ground and wail, my own voice come to me, yelling at me, saying *no, no, no, no. NO.*

And I run off, though I got no idea where I'm going.

MOST OF US sleep next to a cornfield after wrapping up the show and then traveling half the night. Don't nobody like it, but nobody got the gumption to put up a fuss. Some sleep in the trucks and cars, some in a barn about a mile away where the farmer do them the kindness of bedding them down with his horses for the price of a clean hotel room.

I wake up early. The morning still quiet and fresh and dewy, nobody stirring. And the sky clear and blue. I find a little patch of hickory trees got a stream running through and go down there and splash a little water on my face. Then I step out on the road.

Way off down the road a black dot show up in the corn. It come closer and closer, till it finally get to where I can see it's a car. It's too damp to raise a cloud of dust, but when it get close a flock of starlings rise up out of the cornfields and twist around and fly off. The car stop on the roadside up where the motor trucks sitting, and Conger, Fleet, and a couple of roustabouts tumble out.

Fleet see me down by the stream and hurry down hisself.

His eyes look wild, but not like he been drinking. "Lou, you seen Haines or any of them was with him? They show up here?"

I start up like I expect Haines and the rest to be lazing around here somewhere. But the look Fleet give me go right through me and make that smart remark die on my tongue.

"Speak up, gal! You *seen* any of them? Haines? Antoinette? Or Lil, Svetlana, the German?"

"I don't know where them fools—"

"Listen to me," Fleet say, squashing my arms his grip so tight. "Car they was in never got here. We found it broke down ten miles back, but ain't no sign of nobody that was in it."

42

"Maybe they off somewhere listening to the Flat Street Jass—"

He turn his face away like he in pain, and that stop me. Then he look hard at me and say slow, like he talking to a child, "Lou, you *know* things been worse lately. You know they been killing colored men still in *uniform*, and it don't even matter to them. It ain't no time for fooling when a bunch of colored and white show people together go missing in the middle of the night. Now what you know about that car, Lou? I *know* you know something. Tell it now."

Back of where we standing, people waking up and getting the news, a commotion getting started. Voices bouncing off the motor trucks, worried, scared.

"Why you picking on me?" I say.

Fleet let me go. He look me up to the top, down to the bottom, and back again. His eyes get narrow.

"You got a hand in this, ain't you?" he ask me.

I don't say nothing.

"What you done, Lou? What you done?"

He shaking his head like he telling hisself *no* same time as his eyes are telling him *yes* and backing up from me all the while. Then he stop and just stare.

"You messed with that car, ain't you?" he finally ask. "That's why it broke down. That's what you done, ain't it?"

Ain't no point denying it, so I don't. What I was hoping was that that fool Haines, too dumb to find his own dick in the dark, would get hisself so lost when he got back on the road that him and that freak gal would wind up in Mexico.

Fleet put his hands on his hips and stare at me. "Louise," he say, shaking his gray head like he can barely move it.

But he don't say nothing else. Instead, he walk off into the middle of Doc Bell's people, and soon another group pile into two cars and drive off again, one up the road and one back down the way the first just come. Not a one of them look my way.

Kidwell, on his crutch, and Fannie, standing under a hickory tree, stare at me like something dead they found in the cistern, poisoning the water.

Haines's simple face and his easy ways and his good hands try to push theirself into my head then, but I push them right back out again. Med show life ain't for some, and that boy better off where he is, trysting with some gal or drinking moonshine. And that water-head gal sure to end up in a loony bin where she belong. I hear the birds up above, chirping pretty as you please to start a brand-new day. I ain't heard the birds singing in quite a while, and they sure sound sweet to me.

When I go sit down under a tree by myself to enjoy the morning, Fleet come into my head. I can hear that low, steady voice of his riding those slow notes from his banjo right along with the birdsong.

Oh, her name is Ludie Bailey,
And she's coming back to me.
She will have no other lover,
She is coming back to me.
When we leave here in the morning,
Two of us, you'll no more see.

All this time I was wont to think how strange it was that two-timing Ludie Bailey did come back. Now it strike me as strange that her man take her back after what she done.

Yes, he take her. And I wonder how that taking go.

THE CALLING

Oscar Sauer

IT TAKES Sauer over twenty minutes to find the place. The hasty directions he has from Felix Conger turn out to be wrong, and he circles through the same dirt streets of Borden, Pennsylvania, again and again, searching fruitlessly. It's a typical rural hamlet, a Main Street with a few storefronts, two or three fine houses with porches under elms, and then the rest: weather-beaten cottages, low brick hovels, vines and puddles, leaning fences, strays, and too few people to tend it all. Finally he pauses, wipes the sweat from his brow with his shirtsleeve and peers down the unpromising route before him, this lumpy and pitted Granaman Street, barely more than an alley. Not a single horse and wagon, much less a car, has passed him all morning. He walks on, watching as Granaman Street peters out to shacks and the empty shell of a cooper's shop before giving way to fields.

The boardinghouse lies another half-mile on, through waist-high grasses from which birds shoot up as he goes by. When Sauer pauses at the gate of a fence around a yard pounded clean of grass and weeds alike, a fat woman sitting on the porch calls out to him, "You looking for somebody?"

Sauer squints at her, at the way her stomach spills asymmetrically across her lap like an eruption. She is small-boned, giving her an incongruous delicacy. From under her gingham dress poke three stout legs, two white and one blackened. Sauer stares at them until the woman heaves herself up, revealing the third leg to be a coffeepot sitting at her feet.

"Antoinette Riddick," he says.

The woman yanks a thumb over her shoulder. "She got the back room. You can go on around there."

Sauer obeys and follows where she pointed. The fence runs only a few yards along the side of the house, a hulk of unpainted boards that rises, somehow, to two stories. He passes a gaggle of chickens flapping and bickering over a few kernels of corn. Farther on, he skirts a dark maw that is probably an old opening to a cold cellar. Around back are rusting scythes, harrows, halters but no horses. Country people, he has observed when his surroundings intruded on his thoughts, seemed to go out of their way to collect busted and broken things. He toes the rough edge of one of the scythes and imagines the damage it could do to flesh in the dark.

A room, little more than a hovel, juts off the body of the house. The lighting inside will be poor. He'll find dank air, likely a dirt floor, furnishings fit for a junk heap. These places, where "Doc" Bell lodged his Negro performers, were a step above stables, sometimes not even that. Once Sauer would have disdained to examine a patient in such environs. Now, though, he doesn't hesitate. He knocks, says, "Sauer" loudly, and opens the flimsy door.

When the light hits her, the woman inside shields her eyes with one hand.

She sits on a pallet against the wall, burlap stuffed with straw, doubtless full of ticks. Her tremendous head, swollen from hydrocephaly, sways slightly above her shoulders. A turban covers it without hiding its fantastic proportions, which no longer gather in Sauer's attention as they did when he first saw her. He's grown accustomed. The floor, miraculously, is boarded. In the corner a fat candle burns, adding little to the scant light from a single high, crooked window.

There is no other furniture, not even a table. Sauer sets his medical bag on the floor, kneels down, and opens the clasp. "I don't have long," he says. "We have to open the parlor at nine o'clock."

As he picks through his instruments, she asks, "What parlor?"

He blinks at her. It amazes him, what she doesn't know. And what she does. But sitting in a tent half the night, entertaining gawkers who've come to see a freak show, then left alone in some rented room all day, how would she know about the "medical parlor"? There, people who'd bought "medicine" at "Doc" Bell's show the night before gathered for the free "examinations" promised on tickets that came with their soaps, salves, or tonics. He, Oscar Sauer, was the "licensed physician" who looked them over, listened to them complain, and prescribed even more of Bell's useless products.

"That Felix Conger, he finds a room or two to rent cheap," Sauer says. He tells her the rest in vague terms that, he suspects, only make it all seem even worse. He is standing by the time he is finished, wiping an earpiece of his stethoscope with a towel from his bag.

He waits for her disdain, her disgust at him for partaking in such a charade. Unlike Bell, or "Doc" Bell as the man fashions himself, Sauer has delivered babies, removed inflamed tonsils from the throats of sleeping patients. That he does none of these anymore is no excuse.

But she says nothing about it at all. "Would you get me some water?" she asks.

He looks around. There's no pitcher, no basin, not even a glass. It cannot help her condition to live like this. Yet he merely steps to the door, opens it, and looks around until he finds a well at the rear of the yard, near the serrated remains of a brick wall.

He drops the bucket on its rope, draws it up, and then unties it. On his way back, bucket in hand, he finds the proprietress and demands a chair, which she seems shocked to be asked for.

Back inside, he helps Antoinette into the chair and holds the bucket while she cups water with her hands and drinks. Once, twice, thrice, and then she wipes her mouth with her hand. He sits the bucket near the head of the cot, where she can use it later to bathe. If she can't provide a basin, the fat owner will have to find another pail for her well.

He need not ask Antoinette *How is it*, because he knows all about it: The slight spinal deformity that skews her hips, giving her a halting gait. The heavy breathing from pulmonary abnormalities. The neuropathologies. The hydrocephaly itself—water on the brain, laymen call it—the source of all the rest, usually fatal in infancy, rare in one, like her, over the age of twenty. Somehow she has lingered like this, holding on for years.

They begin as usual. She unbuttons the back of her cotton frock with surprising dexterity. She drops it from her shoulders with no modesty. "Breathe," he says, pressing the silver disk of his stethoscope to her back, and she does. Three breaths, a pause while he shifts his instrument, three more breaths. He does not have to tell her. He palpates lymph nodes, probing for signs of infection. There is none. He tests reflexes, wrist, elbow, knee, with his rubber mallet. Neither of them speaks as he proceeds slowly through the steps. In the quiet, through the ritual motions, he can almost forget what he has become.

He uses the candle to look down her throat, but in the poor light, there is little to see. He holds the flame up to check the dilation of her pupils. This test for nervous degeneration, he performs last. The pupils react in tandem. He sets the candle down, puts his implements back in their bag, and snaps the hinges shut.

"You are getting food?" he asks. He knows better than to assume.

"Enough," she says.

He's at the door now, one hand on the loop of twine that serves as a handle. She's staring at him. She does it often, without asking him anything, without speaking at all. He knows how it unnerves some of Bell's people, because a few have told him. That, and her deformity, make them shun her like a witch. It was one of them, Sauer suspects, who sabotaged the car carrying her, Sauer, and three others, stranding them on a deserted road for hours. The driver, who went off to find help, has not been seen in the weeks since.

Just as he pulls the door, she speaks.

"Come back tomorrow."

He frowns. He comes to her every five days, or six, sometimes every week. That is how it has been for months now, since she joined Bell's show in the spring.

She sits staring at him, waiting.

"Yes, tomorrow," Sauer finally says. If she wishes, they will perform the ritual again the next morning, even the one after. He has nothing better to do. He turns away and steps out into the bright day.

SHE IS NOT his concern, really. He bears no responsibility, medical or otherwise, for her. His only relation to her is casual, accidental even. Back in the spring, when Sauer had not been long with the show himself, Felix Conger had demanded that Sauer look over a woman and determine whether she was healthy enough to be an "exhibit" in the show. That was all Conger told him, and Sauer didn't ask for details. They drove out to a field where an old hospital ambulance was parked. Three figures sat waiting inside. A man dressed like a hospital orderly and a stern-faced nurse got out and spoke briefly to Conger. The day was raw, the roadside wormy from a hard rain the night before. Conger opened the door of the ambulance and beckoned him over. His examination, Sauer realized when he blinked away enough of his morning haze, was to be conducted outdoors, right there at the side of the muddy road, the way you might look over a hog for sale. He did not object.

"Just sitting around, is all it takes," Conger had said, tapping his polished shoe impatiently. "Wish I could have it so easy."

Sauer had merely glanced at her at first, expecting some tubercular ne'er-do-well no worse off than the rest of Bell's lot. Then the woman in the car had lifted her gaudy black hat and Sauer had stared in earnest. Even in his fogged state, he felt his breath stop at the sight of such gross cranial distension, such anarchy in a living human form.

"Well?" Conger had snapped, checking his watch to emphasize that he didn't have all day for this.

Sauer had collected himself and performed a quick, cursory examination. Through it all, the woman had not complained or said anything at all, though he found her watching him when he least expected it. He fumbled through as if it had been six years, rather than six months, since he'd last practiced medicine.

"Right now," he had finally reported to Conger, "yes. Tomorrow, who knows?"

He'd been relieved when it was over and Conger dismissed him with a backhand wave. A week later, though, he was at the door to her boardinghouse room. Most days, at that hour, he'd have been sitting in his own room with a bottle in his lap, watching light rise around him like the curtains of a play he did not wish to watch. Instead, standing at her door, he had knocked, heard nothing, knocked again, and gotten no reply, leading him to think the worst. But when he opened the door, she was sitting up already, wearing a faded blue turban. Almost as if she had been expecting him, she did not ask him to explain himself or to leave, either. And as he went through the motions he would repeat on many mornings after, he did not even think to ask her what misfortune had delivered her into Bell's employ.

And so they had fallen into it, this pattern, like a doctor and patient, but not that, because it could not be that for either of them.

She must have understood the inevitability of it ending, he told himself. And yet, gradually, he had gone from expecting not to find her sitting in her room to anticipating her there, waiting in the half-light of curtains drawn to relieve her eyes, turning her dark gaze upon him. Making him pause a moment on the threshold. After a while, after he'd come enough times, he forgot just how unlikely her survival was.

BY MID-MORNING, Sauer peers through the curtain dividing the two rooms Felix Conger has rented in town for the "medical parlor" and sees a mob. Rangy farmers in overalls, doughy women in calico, children crawling over laps and between chair legs, even a pair of Negroes standing over by the door. For the last hour, he's heard a woman's voice cackle over and over, "Half of Borden must be in here!" Borden. In all of his life in Philadelphia, he'd never heard of any Borden. Now he would be spending a week, maybe a week and a half, learning of the warts and piles and female troubles that afflicted the people in and around it. A jumble of small miseries, rising like a wall around him, shielding him from what he does not wish to think about: the life he used to lead. He makes no haste, rushes nobody, and more than a few smile at him in gratitude for what they mistake as patience.

A toothless crone in a white bonnet complains that her fingernails are falling out. She must be ninety, Sauer guesses. She's lucky to have functioning hands at all. He prescribes Doc Bell's Columbium Compound and she buys three bottles.

Three Italians, swarthy from the sun, come in together, gabbling in their language. One tells Sauer in broken English that they are tired. He looks them over briefly. Their hands are too calloused to close in fists, and their cotton pants hang from them. A bottle of VIM-TANA herbal tonic for each of them.

A woman in beige muslin spotted with stains. Four children trail her into the room, tugging at her and whining. She has a baby in her arms. "Show him," she commands one of the children, and a straw-haired boy sitting on the floor draws up his pants legs, revealing heat rash bordering on leprosy. Sauer sells her three tins of Doc Bell's Septo-Soline Salve and gives her the fourth tin for free.

They blur before noon. Faces, stories, ailments. Sauer remembers he never ate breakfast, and then that thought slides away from him along with most others. Having sent the latest patient out, he is about to get up and call in the next when the curtain parts and a short Negro man steps inside the room.

Sauer doesn't bother to reprimand him. He nods slightly at the chair across the small table behind which he sits. There's another table, a white enamel one, against the wall, on it a tray with silver instruments. Next to that, a rolling frame with a pale green curtain. All of these are props. None of the patients have ever questioned why Sauer made no use of them. But this man, instead of sitting, walks over and looks at the instruments.

Seeing this, Sauer watches him more carefully. Felix Conger has warned him that there are Pure Food and Drug agents about, making arrests, closing down medicine shows. But this man is a Negro; impossible that he is a federal agent.

The man walks back and stands before him. He is barely more than five feet tall, but well dressed in pressed shirt and trousers and a light coat, orange-haired, freckled and bespectacled.

"I would like a private audience with the woman you have traveling with you," he says. "The hydrocephalic. The rumors are true? It's not a hoax? How old is she?"

Sauer sits back in his chair. "This is a medical office," he says.

The man produces a card, which has been in his hand all the while, and places it on the table in front of Sauer. *Linus K. Jefferson, M.D.*, it says in elaborate script. *General Practice*. Below that is an address. Sauer puts it down on the table again when he's read it.

Linus Jefferson clears his throat. "My interest is purely scientific. Possibly I can help her. I would have to see her."

52

He isn't the first to ask, Sauer knows. Whole delegations have shown up, far more illustrious committees than this lone Negro doctor, and spoken to Bell or Conger, who have refused every one of them.

"There is nothing anybody can do," Sauer says.

He knows the usual course. The ventricles swelling with cerebro-spinal fluid that could not escape the cranium, the nervous functions squeezed and twisted into chaos. Paralysis, respiratory failure. Sauer had seen only a few other cases, babies who died within the week of his examination, before her. The question is not how Antoinette might be helped, but why she is alive at all.

Linus Jefferson looks around the room once more. "Medical progress," he says, his voice hard-edged, "may take root where you least expect it. Please give her my assurances that my services are of the highest standards." He looks at Sauer. "I can provide references, if she wishes to see them. Very good ones."

But Sauer has, by now, grown tired of Linus Jefferson. There are patients waiting. He can hear the blurry clamor from the next room. He turns to the ledger lying open on his table and begins writing on the next blank line.

After a few moments, a whisper of curtain alerts him that Linus Jefferson is gone, that the next patient has come to him. Sauer looks up and finds his wife across the room from him. Greta, in one of her gauzy summer frocks, soft with gathered fabric, her ankles showing the pale lisle stockings she favors, her hand raised in the air as if she seeks to grasp his thoughts as they float inevitably toward her.

Sauer makes his eyes close. Waits, breathing heavily.

When he looks again, the woman walking toward him is what he knows she must be: not his wife, Greta, just a local woman of some grace with a ticket in her hand. Greta is dead. Sauer looks down at the ledger page, the spillage of words there, and goes back to his work.

THE NEXT morning, Sauer wakes up in the clothes he went to sleep in, runs his fingers through his thinning hair, throws a splash of water across his face, and sets out across Borden for the visit he promised to Antoinette. The only remnants of his night of drinking are a blurring of his senses and the smell of whiskey in his shirt and trousers. He hasn't been drunk. True stupid drunkenness eludes him. Enough whiskey, especially the whip-crack moonshine he's been reduced to because of wartime shortages and the wartime prohibition, and he simply passes out.

In soft focus, its morning sounds hazed, Borden is almost pleasant. Sauer makes his way down a street fitted with small houses, warehouses, and sheds. Outside one shed, a woman and three men load brooms into a two-horse wagon. From another comes the distant metal clanging of machinery. Oily puddles glow at him as Sauer walks roadside.

At the boardinghouse, the three-legged woman is absent, the porch empty. Just as well, as he would no more have seen her clearly this morning than the prior one. Enough whiskey, and his memories of last fall's Spanish influenza epidemic began to blend into the green swells and valleys of the Pennsylvania countryside. The makeshift Philadelphia armory sick wards, the faces of the stricken, their skin blue-black from cyanosis, their lips specked with sputum gurgling up from their lungs, all of it slipped and flickered among the sheets of mist that shrouded the fields of corn and wheat and barley in the vacant hours of early morning. And the voices of his dying patients, calling to him for help he could not give, begging, pleading, the voices became the dawn chatter of birds. For such relief, he'll run the risk that a stray batch of home brew will turn out to be poison.

Around the back of the house, there are no chickens today. A pig standing under a maple sapling seems to watch him sullenly. The door to the rear room stands open.

She is there, waiting for him. Already wearing the wide-brimmed, beribboned black hat, already shod. Sauer pauses in the doorway. This is not what he expected. He had thought she wanted him to monitor her more closely. But she looks like a woman prepared to head off to market.

He hesitates, rakes his fingers through his hair, and steps in.

"I want to see him," she says, holding out something to him.

A slip of paper? No. He recognizes at once what he saw just yesterday, even with his eyes half out of focus. It is the card of the orange-haired Negro doctor, Jefferson. How did she get it? Had the man had the temerity to pay a visit to her sideshow tent after speaking to Sauer?

He sits his black bag on the floor and slowly rolls up first one sleeve, then the other. He will have to tell her that it would be a mistake to allow the self-absorbed Linus Jefferson, or any of the other pompous fools who have sought her, to amuse themselves with a novel specimen. He will have to tell her what doctors like Linus Jefferson will do. Bring colleagues to stare at her naked. Draw blood, mucous, even bits of flesh, to satisfy some stupid pet theory that a sensible layperson would dismiss, and Sauer should know. He has taken part in such travesties himself. Not long after the Spanish flu arrived, before anyone knew what manner of dying awaited them all, before the weekly death tolls for Philadelphia alone climbed into the hundreds, he'd stopped at the bed of a wheezing woman and bade a medical student lean close and note the distinctive, telltale rattle of her dying breath.

"Did Bell tell you that you must do this?" he begins slowly. "Did Conger?"

"No," she says.

The haze from the whiskey is lifting. He looks into the shifting dark of her eyes, looks away again.

"This Jefferson is just—" Sauer begins.

"I know what he is," Antoinette says.

She is abrupt, but Sauer does not bother to take offense. He looks at her slender shoulders, at the mesh roses and curls of ribbon that dangle from the brim of the black straw hat that she uses to hide her deformity in public, and wonders what milliner fashioned such a thing for her. "Listen to me," he says wearily.

But she does not listen. She struggles to her feet and comes closer and pins him with her dark eyes and talks instead. "Headache powders don't work now. It's like some kind of electric light is burning up in my head all the time." She pauses as if she wants to be sure he hears.

It is more than she has ever said to him. Even so, Sauer can make no sense of it.

She doesn't wait for him. "I can't catch my breath no matter how long I rest. You understand me?"

The room feels suddenly close. Sauer backs away, all the way to the open door. He clears his throat, but finds he has nothing to say. For he is coming to understand what she is talking about. Her condition has worsened. Why didn't she tell him before now? But why should she have? What good would it have done her? Still it is a shock to him, the suddenness of the onset, the way he missed all of the signs.

He steps onto the threshold. Outside, green fields drowse in the sunshine, clouds bump each other lazily in the sky. He turns back and finds her gazing past him at the same fields and sky. There is no resignation in her face at all, no concession to the inevitability of what awaits her. Then she turns her face to him and her eyes, made small and close by the swelling of her cranium the hat cannot fully mask, find him again.

"Will you bring a car?" she asks. "One of Bell's?"

"A car?" he echoes, confused. What use would she have—but then he understands, finally, what she has asked him here for. It is nothing to do with Conger or Bell at all, what they might want or allow. He looks down at the card he still holds, at Linus Jefferson's address in a town he has never heard of, printed in bold black letters. It is Sauer's help that she wants.

He turns away. The high heat of afternoon, still hours away, suddenly seems to suffuse him. "I must go. I must—I am late to open the parlor, and, and...people are waiting for..."

He ceases muttering and steps out into the yard, but he can feel her gaze on him, grabbing him like a hand.

Not until he has reached the vacant cooper's shop, where he has to stop to catch his breath after the pace he has kept up, does he remember. He left his doctor's bag in her room. He contemplates, for a moment, going back to get it, then decides not to. Where he is going, he will not need it.

BACK IN TOWN, he keeps the parlor running for one hour, two, three, then well past the time when Felix Conger has instructed him to close for the day. "Keeps up demand," Conger has said to him, "when people can't get what they want easy." But that is not Sauer's concern today. He allows the procession of "patients" to continue, a welcome monotony, until a rail-thin, sun-spotted farmer in cap and overalls enters and sits gingerly across from him.

The man purses chapped lips, squints, and complains of being always tired. Sauer half-listens until the man stands, drops the overalls off his shoulders and pulls up his shirt. On his back, under the ledge of his lowest rib, rises a round, tumorous bulge. The man's fingers prod it, assuring Sauer of its solidity. His own fingers, in fact, burn at the sight of it. A solid mass. He stares at it.

"How long has it been there?" he asks.

The man smiles and says he doesn't remember, then rattles on about how coffee and molasses, in particular, taste peculiar to him these last few weeks. And he's got a bad tooth in back, too. On and on. Clearly he has no idea of the seriousness of the growth on his back.

"What's that?" the farmer says, scratching his ear. "What you saying?"

Sauer sits forward in his chair, his fists clenched on the table in front of him. This is not the script. The pitch he is supposed to make for Bell's pills or salves or tonics. He knows the rules that Bell has laid down, the ones that will keep the show out of trouble, keep the money coming in: Do not touch any patients, which is evidence of a real examination that could leave Bell liable for a misdiagnosis; do not offer a clear diagnosis; suggest Bell's products, but do not promise that any of them will cure a thing. They "treat" nervous exhaustion, or female troubles, or catarrh, or piles. As long as he stayed within these limits, Bell and Conger could keep any meddling authorities at bay, could keep the show clattering along the rural back roads that sustained it. Sauer looks down at the tabletop, wishing this farmer would simply get up and take his tumor somewhere else. But of course, he does not.

Sauer comes over and turns the man sideways. "Move your hands," he says. He yanks the clothes from the spot on the man's back, tearing the shirt where it catches on a buckle, and palpates the growth. Immediately, he can feel the movement of a larger mass below the surface, the hold of a malignancy rooted and thriving where it does not belong.

Sauer drops the shirt and steps back a few paces. His face, he can feel, is flushed. His hand tingles as if the blood has rushed back into it after a long absence. The farmer, after the sudden commands and rough handling, stands there looking perplexed. He grins and scratches a stubbly cheek, then he looks serious, then he grins again.

"Well, Doc, what you think?" he asks.

Sauer glares at him. "Go to a doctor," he says. He nods at the small square of Borden visible through the shaded window behind him, ignoring the irony in what he has just said when the farmer frowns confusedly at Sauer's white lab coat. "You have a tumor. Get it cut out before it kills you."

The farmer's pinched face blanches. "You telling me—"

"Go and do it *now*," Sauer says.

The farmer snatches up his cap and scurries out of the room.

Sauer stands there, breathing hard, staring at the red-and-white-checked curtain through which the man has disappeared. He can hear the buzz of other people talking as they wait. A room full, still, though it is late afternoon now. He doubts he will see another like the farmer in Borden. It is unlikely the crowd holds in store a second case like his. But it is not impossible. If the man had not pulled back his own clothes, Sauer would have taken him for just another hypochondriac.

He walks slowly back to the desk and looks at the ledger where he has recorded sales. There are no names, no indications of ailments. Most were complainers, Sauer knows, and almost all the rest suffered the minor ailments that afflicted everyone now and then. Time was the best healer of these. A little of Bell's junk neither helped nor hurt them. But there must have been other sicknesses he did not detect. Cases of asthma, of dropsy, of epilepsy, that passed before him as if he were blind. Cases he did not see because he did not wish to see.

He closes the ledger. What he wants, at this moment, is a bottle of whiskey. The comforting haze. But instead, he steps into the waiting room, closes down the parlor for the day, and walks slowly into the street.

THE CAR Sauer hires takes them to a yellow clapboard house surrounded by a neat picket fence. A sign on the clipped lawn directs them to the rear. Sauer follows Antoinette down a slated path to a small addition built on the back of the house. With dusk an hour away, they will have to hurry to finish here and then get back to the show in time.

Linus Jefferson opens the door before Sauer can knock. A smile flits across his face. He leads them through a small, neat waiting room to a door that opens onto a bright examination room. His job done,

Sauer takes a seat in the paneled waiting room rather than follow. The door swings closed. He reaches into his pants pocket for a flask, and the door swings open again.

"She wants you present," says Linus Jefferson.

Sauer gets up again. It does not matter whether he is sitting in the dim waiting room, a yard from Linus Jefferson, or on the moon. Whatever goes on, he has no role to play in it at all. He has done what she asked, brought her here. He shuffles to the chair Jefferson points him to and sits.

But in spite of himself, he watches Linus Jefferson wash his hands in a small sink, wipe them dry, approach Antoinette where she sits on a low examination table, reach for the black hat that waves slightly with the constant motion of her head. She grabs his wrist before he can touch her.

For a moment, he just stares at her. Then he says, "May I . . . ?" She lets go of his hand. He adjusts his glasses, lifts the hat gently, and sets it on the table beside her. His face grave, he walks slowly around the table, looking at Antoinette from every angle. He crosses his arms. Several times he stops and stares, seemingly thinking something through, but more likely, Sauer guesses, dumbstruck by the extent of her deformity. Dr. Jefferson is not finding this to be quite like the pictures in his textbooks. He is rethinking his arrogant remarks about medical progress. He is thinking, *God in Heaven*, if he is a religious man, and probably even if he is not. All of this Sauer reads in Jefferson's expression and the slow uncertain movement of his feet. But it is more than he wants to know. He looks away from the two of them and sends his gaze roaming randomly around the spotless room.

Some time passes, Sauer does not know how much, before Jefferson draws his attention back by unrolling a measuring tape. He holds it up before his patient, waiting. "Go ahead," Antoinette tells him. Gingerly, he wraps it around her cranium and pinches two ends together lightly on her forehead. He scribbles on a pad beside him. It is a series of dexterous movements. Jefferson, Sauer imagines, is over his initial shock.

He looks at a vase across the room, its neck blooming with wildflowers. Tiger lilies. On the wall hang diplomas, their lettering too small for Sauer to read. The frames gleam. They've been polished recently. On the desk is a small wooden nameplate that reads *Linus K. Jefferson, M.D.* in the same lettering as appears on the card, this time in brass.

A medical history. Jefferson is taking a medical history, and Sauer hears fragments of the questions though he tries not to listen. *Does anyone in your family have heart problems...Did your mother have a difficult pregnancy...At what age...attempts to relieve the pressure...diphtheria...malaria...scarlet fever...* And Antoinette's voice, steady, flat, answering each of the questions so briefly that a silence descends on the room before Linus Jefferson gets the next one out of his mouth.

"Is anyone else, er, are there cases of imbecility in your family?"

Jefferson is scribbling on his pad when he asks this. It is several moments before he looks up, frowning through his glasses, at the lack of a quick answer.

Antoinette is staring at him. "You don't know a thing, do you?" she asks.

Jefferson's pencil, which he has placed on his pad, rolls off and falls on the floor with a clatter.

"Pardon me?" he asks.

"You don't know anything," Antoinette says, and this time it is not a question. She begins to slide herself forward, off the table.

Jefferson throws an alarmed look at Sauer, then raises his hand to restrain Antoinette, and then seems to think better of it. She puts her hat back on.

"Let's go," she says to Sauer.

Sauer stands, relieved it is over with. Linus Jefferson makes no attempt to stop them as Sauer follows Antoinette back through the waiting room and outside, this time into gathering dusk. Sauer told the car he hired to come back in half an hour. Already it has been longer than that. He hopes the driver has waited. They are already too late to reach the show in time, and he will have to make explanations to Felix Conger, maybe even to Bell himself, about why "Sheba, Queen of the Nile" was absent from her tent. It will not be pleasant. Conger, notoriously short-tempered, once told him to remember, boozers like him who'd lost their practices were a dime a dozen. Any decent-sized saloon was sure to shelter one or two. If he wanted to, he could replace Sauer in ten minutes. Maybe less.

With lightning bugs winking through the cool air around him, Sauer feels an urge to close his eyes, raise his face to the imminent stars, move unseen as he used to when he took long walks through the streets of Philadelphia at night after closing his practice for the day. Greta fretted and worried that he would get hit in the head and robbed, but nothing ever happened to him. In fact, when people began to die, when the Spanish flu culled his patients as relentlessly as a gardener pulling weeds, when Greta herself began to cough and wheeze, Sauer did not develop so much as a sniffle.

Behind him, he hears Antoinette's rough breathing, audible over the noise of the singing crickets in the fields around them. In spite of himself, he turns to look and sees her, a dark shape against the dimming yellow wall behind her. She has stopped to lean heavily on the picket fence only a few yards from the house. It will not be long before the darkness engulfs her.

He turns and goes back to her and offers her his arm, something he has not done before. "Come, we must go, now," he says. "Come with me."

Up on the road, the lamps of the waiting car cut on and throw columns of light down the road.

THE FOLLOWING afternoon, Sauer finds himself in Peanut Louie's Saloon. It's a small place with tall front windows. The room itself, wrapped around the bar, forms an L. Sauer shouldn't be here. It's not good business for the show's doctor to be seen frequenting saloons, but he no longer gives a damn. He takes a stool at the end of the bar.

The bartender, a short man with black hair slicked to his head, approaches wiping a glass with a white rag. "We're dry with the war prohibition," he says, "except for weak beer. What'll it be?"

Sauer asks for lemonade, and when it's in front of him, he takes out his flask and tops off the glass. The bartender watches briefly, appears to think better of saying anything, and walks away.

The men farther down the bar, and scattered among the tables, wear shirts and trousers stained with dirt or oil. Some have their sleeves rolled up, as they likely did while working. None of them wear a hat. Mill workers, farm laborers, a mechanic or two, Sauer guesses.

"Ain't you with that med show?" the bartender, back in front of Sauer, chooses that moment to ask.

Sauer says nothing.

"Better hit the road when you down that," says the bartender, his voice low.

Behind Sauer, a conversation wanders pointlessly.

"Willard shoulda won. It was low blows that sunk him."

"Aw, c'mon, Dempsey won it fair and square."

"You think them steel workers gonna strike?"

"Nothing but a bunch of filthy Reds!"

"They ain't all bad! Cousin of mine—"

"Worst thing is they bring in niggers to scab."

"Naw! They got plenty of hunkies for that."

"I like them hunky gals, though. They talk funny, but they..."

Sauer drinks the whole glass and refills it with straight whiskey. He ignores the bartender's more frequent glances. The idiot banter, the alcohol, the late afternoon sun slanting through the dusty windows, all of it reminds him he is not in Philadelphia. Out here, in farm country, there had been less death. In Philadelphia the bodies had piled up. The morgue overflowed, then its halls. After a while, the authorities left people where they died. Gravediggers refused work. Out here, out in the middle of nowhere, there was ground enough to absorb the dead. Prayers, flowers, graves for all of them, and that made many fewer ghosts.

After he has swallowed the last of his glass, he considers refilling it and decides not to. It isn't working. The farmer with the tumor, Linus Jefferson and his shaking hands, the silhouette of Antoinette in the twilight, all of them are sharp and clear in his mind. When she took his arm, the weight was not ghostly light but heavy and lingering. After settling her in the backseat of the car, he'd stood there until the driver barked, "Buddy, I ain't got all night!"

"Hey," says a local, who's taken a barstool a few seats from Sauer.

Sauer ignores him.

"Say, you got a light?"

Sauer ignores him.

"Hey, I'm talking to you!" The man has a hand on his arm now, wiry fingers coiled tight. His little eyes shine bright with offense.

Sauer shrugs him off, not hard enough to tip him, but the man falls on the floor anyway. The sound is like an armful of potatoes dropped on a tabletop. Sauer is lifting his glass to his lips when a fist crashes into his left ear.

It's the same local, up on his feet again, one eye drooping, his face twisted in rage. Sauer ducks off the barstool before he can land a second blow, and the man falls across the stool. Sauer grasps his shirt and throws him head-first onto the floor. The man reaches out for Sauer's leg, and Sauer looks down at him, knowing he should stop. But he doesn't. He steps over the groping hand, moving swiftly now, and kicks the man in the ribs. A gargling cry rings through the room. He kicks again. The man writhes.

That is enough. Sauer knows he should stop. But he does not. He drops to one knee and reaches for the bloody, crumpled body. Around him he can feel a congregation of others, watching him but doing nothing to stop him. His fingers lock around the slick, bruised throat. His grip tightens. But staring into that stupid face, the one he is consumed with the thought of smashing, he finds he cannot do what he wants to do. It is something in the face. He peers closer, looking for it. The face is nothing extraordinary. Narrow forehead, bony nose, stubble like a rash swarming across the jawline. Then Sauer finds it, what is calling out to him. There's no rise and fall of the chest, no whistle of wind through the nose. The skin, where it shows through the smears of blood, is bluish.

His hands move ahead of his thoughts. In an instant they have the mouth open, the wet, pink hole gaping empty. He slides a finger in, finds the clogged tongue, and lifts it up out of the throat. The man does not awaken, but he draws a breath, a long, ragged, living gasp.

Sauer unbuttons the bloody shirt, puts his ear near the crooked lips. The breath comes strongly and evenly now. He clears the dirty hair away from the bruised eye and parts the lids with his thumb and index finger. The eye is still intact, salvageable with ice and some modest attention. The hands. There is a dislocated thumb. He lifts the hand and forces the knuckle back into place.

Nobody stops him. They stand around, watching, as he waits for some of them to pull him off and drag him away. But they do not, and so he continues, loosening the shirt further, lightly examining the thin arms for fractures. All that remains is the gash across the forehead, the cut itself invisible but rich with blood that flows like a tide down the side of the head.

Sauer looks up. A circle of faces surrounds him, staring. Hovering in the dusty air, their eyes wide, wet, fixed on him. One has a nose so flint-thin his nostrils flutter and flare with every breath. Another, skin as granular as new snow.

"Bartender," Sauer says, "bring me water and a clean towel."

He will do what he can.

The Schenectady Girls

Matilda "Tildy" South

MANY A day at the Kensalls' place, I looked up from cooking and there was a blue jay sitting in the tree outside the kitchen window. Nothing special, just some bones and blue feathers and beady eyes, but I liked him just the same. After a while I started thinking he stopped by just to see me, and it made the work a little easier. But then the missus would come in and say, Matilda, the baby need changing. Or the mister would show up and say, Matilda, come on upstairs and shine my shoes for me. And the blue jay flew off, like he didn't like it any more than I did.

I took off from there just about when they was saying there was a war across the ocean. Just when we was first hearing about what them Huns was up to. I know it looked crazy, taking off in such times. I know the Kensalls wasn't no different really from a thousand others just like them, and I seen plenty enough of them in my thirty-seven years on this earth to know that. But nobody ever said I lacked for sense, and it was sense that said to me, Tildy, this here is no life to be waking up to every morning. And so I run off.

I hadn't never done that before, quitting a regular job. Not when I got cheated of my wages, not when the work was twice what they said, not when I got bit by a dog, not when sickness in a house nearly killed me. Only way I lost a job was when they let me go, and then I went knocking at every door for another spot. And I got one in time. Always was plenty of white folks who didn't take to raising their own babies any more than they did to cooking and cleaning. Some was kinder than others, but none was ever nobody I wanted for a friend.

That Mr. Kensall, though, when he come up on me quiet while I was making biscuits and pressed himself up against me, I said to myself, No sir. Maybe I ain't cut out for this kind of work. Maybe I'm crazy to leave a regular spot, but I got to try something new.

TONIGHT GONNA be our last in this place, and ain't nobody sorry for it but me. Doc Bell's people been complaining all week long about this and that little thing. Saying there ain't enough of a town here to have a post office, a funeral parlor, a doghouse, or even a dump. Saying people coming out to the shows hold on to their money so tight you got to kill 'em to get it loose. Men stupid as cows. Ugly children. Folks been that way, full of sour and spite, ever since that fella Haines disappeared, and the weather don't make them no sunnier. Ain't been fit for drowning kittens much less putting on a show every night. If it wasn't for the heat, you wouldn't even know it was summer. Seem like there's a cloud hanging over Midlow, Pennsylvania, that never run out of water.

But Midlow is fine by me. The people seem kind of sad here. They just sit and watch whenever I come out, and they don't call out no wise remarks or fidget around and keep up their talking like people in some places do. The ice pick gets them all watching me. Then I do the poker. Then I do the sword with the fancy handle full of phony diamonds and rubies and emeralds, and some of them let off little gasps and *ahhh*s and squeals like they know how it feel to swallow something that don't belong in your body.

Marie say, Tildy, don't it hurt? Don't you cough up blood? Don't you get stomach trouble? And her eyes crunch up and she shiver and shake her head like she could never, ever even try a thing like that herself. But the man that showed me how, he said you just got to practice till your throat give up gagging. And you got to hold still no matter what idea creep in your head.

Sometimes it strike me how far I come from that Kensall kind of life. It do feel good not having all them white folks telling me what to do every minute of the day. But it do feel strange with Doc Bell, too. Nobody got a hold of my body now, but it do feel strange to find out exactly where the bottom of me is every day. It do feel strange to know that.

Lots of people think it's some kind of trick. Even after Mr. Conger let somebody in the audience hold on to the sword and see it's real, they swear I'm a fake. But these people in Midlow just sit there and watch me while Mr. Conger keep talking and talking about Matilda the Great. After the sword I do a curtain rod. And then a scythe.

There ain't nothing I can't swallow. Doc Bell say I'm downright amazing, the best he ever did see. Way he figure it, he'll be keeping me on for good.

MARIE MAKE things with a needle and cloth. You wouldn't think she could do it, to look at her. One of them milk-white gals, is what people say about her type. Pretty curls, blue eyes, fingers as smooth as water that look like they never do no honest work. But she do plenty of work now. She make all the costumes and she do all the mending, too. She whipped up a new black witchy dress for Madame Svetlana the medium, she done up a bunch of natty suits for Mr. Conger, she even made up a striped Uncle Sam uniform with a top hat and all for Doc Bell, and it ain't just any seamstress that can sew up a suit for a seven-

and-a-half-foot-tall man without batting an eye. And when she ain't sewing for the show, she sew the most beautiful frocks for the two of us. She favor cream colors for herself, pie yellow and blue like the sky, and for me it's all the bows you could want, little bows at the hem or the waist or one sitting between my bosoms like as to say, Look at me. Most often I make her take off the bows. I tell her, homely woman like me can't bring off nothing like that. With all these knees and elbows, hair like some dustball and a face as long as a goat's? You want to make a fool of me? She just laugh and say I got to have something to wear to town. For when I step away from Matilda the Great and into Tildy.

Every day heading up to showtime, she make the rounds with her sewing basket and see to anything that need to be done. Sometimes she take a few minutes, but most often she is gone for hours, seeing to everybody, seeing to everything from rips and tears to loose hems and missing scarves and this person got to have the back taken in a little 'cause they're skinnier now to that one need his pants shortened up 'cause he's tripping over them during the fast part of the act. Most often she is still flitting hither and yon when the show start up at sunset, and it ain't till I get out onstage doing my first number with the pick and the poker that I find out where she is.

Standing out there with the audience is usually where she is, watching us like she ain't a part of Doc Bell's show at all. Like she just come in from the farm, like most of the people, for a bit of entertainment to brighten up the day after day after day of hoeing cabbage and sowing corn and tending to chickens and pigs and cows. She nearly glow at night, my Marie, in her frocks. Standing out there, watching us, laughing and clapping along with the rest of the people.

When I get to the scythe, my Marie turn her eyes away like she can't bear to watch it go down. Many folks do just the same. But when I pull it out and show I ain't sliced up my lungs and kidneys and heart, she got her eyes on me every time.

70

I FIRST SET eyes on her when the show was in Georgia, following the spring weather as it got farther and farther north the way Doc Bell and Mr. Conger done every year I been with them. Going slow so as not to get out in front of the flowers and that spring feeling that make people want to spend their money, Mr. Conger say. We was stopped outside a little town called Shaw and I was in a mill end shop looking for scraps. Back then, before Marie, we did our own handiwork.

She come in with her husband, a white man with a moustache and the coldest eyes you ever did see. They looked at some of the finer bolts of cloth, and she just kept shaking her head, no, no, not this one, not that one neither. He would touch another, and read out the name, Turkish chamois or White Rose taffeta or what have you, and she would hum and tip her head and say, no, not that one. Then they come over to the table where I was sorting through scraps and Marie looked over at me and stuck her hands right in there, too, like she was somebody's help and not a gentleman's wife.

"Marie, come now...," her husband said.

She didn't pay him no mind, so he stepped over to me and said, can I help him. I told him I didn't work there, so off he went, huffing and puffing, to find somebody that did.

She just pulled up pieces and tossed them around for a while, like it was a game, till she was standing near to me and I felt her warmth. It was in the scraps, spreading out like wetness. It went in my fingers and up my arms. It scared me, coming from a white lady, but I didn't move.

"I have not seen you in town before," she said.

"No, ma'am," I said back.

"You are with that traveling medicine show, aren't you?"

In them little towns down south in particular, you got to watch the town folk. No matter if you're white or Negro. They come laugh at you one night and knock you in the head for your own good the next.

But I said yes. And she stepped next to me and touched my hand under the scraps, and I looked in her face and saw all the colors there

71

right under her skin that her husband couldn't see. She wasn't a white lady, she just looked like one.

Then her husband come and take her away, but I was back the next day and so was she. I waited two hours for her. This time she sent him off to fetch her a tin of mints from the dry goods shop down the way.

I hadn't a word in my mouth to say. Not before she spoke, not even when she asked me my name.

THE RAIN just keep falling. Even though we got the big tent up to keep the people dry, they ain't coming out in numbers with the roads a muddy mess, and all of us know we ain't giving them much to see if they do. Seem like our hearts just ain't in the show no more. People been missing cues and flubbing the lines of acts they know in their sleep. Our music got all the right notes, far as I can tell, but it don't sound right somehow, like it's a little too slow or flat. The dancing make you tired to watch it, I heard somebody say. Even that bigmouth Ma Fleet been keeping to herself, keeping quiet, like she want to save up her voice for the stage.

Only Doc Bell seem the same. He do his three lectures a night every night just like always, and once he get started ain't a soul in the audience thinking about the weather. It only take a minute for him to get their minds on themselves, on all the dangers just waiting to take hold of their bodies, on how weak they are, on how much they need some help to make it through this cruel world whole. Stomach troubles. Piles. Nervous troubles. Weak blood. Rheumatism. Soft bones. Liver troubles. Tapeworms. Every few days, on his third lecture, Doc Bell take out a big bottle and tell the people about the worm inside that come out of the belly of a man in Tierra del Fuego in 1863 when the man was twenty-one years old and weighed three hundred pounds because of all the tapeworms he had living inside of him and didn't even know it.

Doc Bell march to one end of the stage and look at them. He got on his Wild West getup tonight, double-breasted suit and vest with a pocket watch chain, string tie and a wing collar. When he whip off the Stetson and his black hair fall in his face, wild is just what he look.

"Them beasts in his bowels robbed him of his vitality! Fatigue, ladies and gentlemen, fatigue became *his constant companion.*"

Doc Bell stride over to the other end of the stage and point that hat at some poor lady in the audience.

"One at a time, *he lost every strand of hair on his head!*"

Then, center stage, he go dead silent for a minute and sweep his eyes over every soul out there, it seem. He pick up that nasty jar with a long white shape coiled up inside it.

"Now gentlemen, hold the ladies' hands! I'm gonna unscrew this here lid and show you *the extent of the evil that can reside in the body of one unawares.*"

He don't get no farther than that before the commotion and fainting bring things to a halt. It never fail to get some people to run up front, waving their money to buy some medicine.

Doc Bell never do take out that tapeworm, and it's a good thing. It ain't nothing but a pillowcase bent and twisted up in a jar of pickling brine.

AFTER THE show, we all packing ourselves into the cars and motor trucks to go back to the boardinghouse and Marie go missing. Dark a night as it is, I know I ain't made no mistake. I watched everybody who got on board, and she ain't there.

Mr. Conger find me waiting on the side of the road.

"You know where she is?" he ask me before I say one word.

We all been jumpy lately, afraid we gonna lose somebody else after that business with the guitar player, but Mr. Conger don't sound worried about Marie, and I know why. This ain't the first time she disappeared. First time, we all ready to go, and ain't no Marie to be seen.

We spent a whole hour beating the bushes looking for her before she come strolling in from a stargazing trip with Madame Svetlana.

I wasn't sore about it. But don't nobody like Madame Svetlana, was the funny part.

Second time, it was the middle of the day, broad daylight. Mr. Kidwell come and find me, and I say Marie got to be about somewhere, but he shake his head and say she ain't. We was ready to send somebody into the town when she come back with that Willie boy and a string of fish, and the two of them looking like perfect country bumpkins. And I know Marie ain't never touched no dead fish, much less a worm, in her life.

The third time, she showed up after a while smiling and keeping her business to herself. She ain't told me yet where she gone. Stop acting like the police, she say when I ask. She ain't no criminal. So I quit asking.

Mr. Conger put his hand on his hip and push his hat back like he gonna see better in the dark that way. I'm waiting for him to say who got to go with me to look for her this time when he take off his hat altogether and slap his leg with it.

"You coming back with us, or you want to stay here and wait for her?" he say like he's good and tired of such foolishness.

At first I think I ain't heard him right.

"You telling me you gonna leave her here?" I ask him.

"Precisely," he say. "She can do her sporting around on her own time."

I look out at them black cornfields, at the show shut down and dark for the night, no laughing, no people, just a lantern or two glowing where somebody's left on watch. It's got to be a good five-mile walk back to the boardinghouse, and that's if she don't take no wrong turns on strange roads.

"You ask me, Matilda," Mr. Conger say, and he got to yell now because the driver got the nearest car running, "you're better off leaving her."

He put his hat back on and stand there, waiting for me to do what he say.

"Well, I didn't ask you," I say back.

He give me a look, but he hop in the car and it start off. Soon as it's gone I check with the roustabouts on watch. Two of them, that boy Willie and the other one that grin all the time, and neither one of them seen her. And they're too busy with a checker game to help me look for Marie, so I set off by myself.

I walk up and down some roads nearby, but I don't see no signs of Marie. I walk out to the edge of a cornfield and stand there, looking in. Corn is a simple thing in the day, nothing but long green leaves and tall stalks and the ears poking out of their husks after a while. But at night you go in there and ain't no sun to tell you your directions, and like as not you will get lost. Don't bother most folks, but sometimes they pull a full-grown fella out of there after a few hours and he ain't himself for a week. Some folks won't go back in after that. Something about being alone in there, about forgetting everything while you are.

You got to stick to your row. That's how I go, straight till I come out on the other side. Then back in, then out, then in again. Marie's husband come into my head while I'm out there, sitting in his wing chair in their parlor, wondering where his wife run off to. He know she run off, because her grip and her clothes are gone from the closet. But he don't know where, or why. He don't look cold-eyed no more to me. He stare at his shoes on the carpet, dirty like he ain't wont to let them get. He look up at the walls, at the shelves full of whatnot Marie brought in that he never looked at before, all them pretty picture frames and golden snuffboxes and porcelain angels and crystal candy dishes and dolls with their hair done up in jewels. He think she surely got to come back to fetch all them pretty things. He think the best thing to do is to wait.

In the middle of a row I hear a whistle that ain't no bird. I want to run after it, but I stop myself. I finish my row, and turn around and go back. And there Willie stand, smoking a cigarette and waiting for me. He forgot to tell me before. Marie hitched a ride back to town with a minister and his family that was at the show.

I thank Willie for his kindness, then start walking.

THE NEXT DAY, Mr. Conger get us all together and tell us Doc Bell want us to change some things, snap it up some to get the people back in droves again in spite of all this rain. First he get Mr. Kidwell up on the stage and tell him he want more of the lush in his Irishman act. Mr. Kidwell try it, and he ain't too limber, what with a sore ankle, but Mr. Conger make him flop over twenty times or more before he give up and shoo Mr. Kidwell off the stage.

Then he send Ma and Pa Fleet up there. Ma Fleet got on the frock she slept in and a head rag that look fit for shining shoes, but she stand right in the middle of the stage like she sporting gold and diamonds anyway. Mr. Conger try to rearrange one of their skits by adding some nonsense about a lost pig. Everybody standing there watching know it ain't funny, but we don't say a word 'cause we all too busy wondering what he got in store for us.

Then Mr. Conger get Mr. Kidwell and a new boy up there with a ukulele and a jug and walk them through a song called "Lorelei" about a lass with curly hair that grow on her head and on her back. Her husband plan to run off when he find out about her back, but he wind up shaving her every winter for wool instead. They get the ukulele notes right off but have no end of trouble with the words. They call the girl "Lulabelle" and "Louisa May" and whatnot because they can't remember "Lorelei."

Mr. Conger get sore about then and throw his bowler on the ground. "You all stink worse than a bunch of dubs!" he yell, and his face get red. He rip off his suit jacket and throw that in the mud, too. "If I was calling the shots, I'd fire every last one of you!"

He walk back and forth a few times, and we all stand there watching him, not saying a word. I'm feeling about as miserable as a lost lamb and I'm starting to think, Maybe folks are right. Maybe this Midlow, Pennsylvania, got some kind of curse on it or something. It's three more days till we pack up and leave this place with its sad-faced people, but I'm ready to go now.

Marie, who been standing by me the whole while and watching, pinch my arm. I don't want to draw Mr. Conger's attention, but I look over at her. She's smiling, of all things.

"At times he reminds me of a monkey that got his peanuts stolen by a mischievous child!" she say, and snort and laugh.

I try to shush her, but it ain't no use. He's looking our way now.

"Marie," he say, "we need new costumes. Lots of them." He turn his head and spit. "You're going to sew till your fingers want to drop off. And you." He look at me. "You're going to need those steady hands for some new stunts I'm working on."

He ain't gonna tell me what they are, though, 'cause he got others to attend to first. It's the acrobats next, both of them, and he punish them for a while till they surely feeling pretty busted up too, and then he get to Madame Svetlana, the medium. Mr. Conger keep it up all afternoon. It start to feel like we're off in France in the war, hunkered down in the mud and the trenches, waiting for the next bomb to blow up some more of us.

Only I ain't like the rest. I can swallow anything, but I ain't like them just the same. Mr. Conger got to do the talking for me 'cause I can't do it myself. The once I tried, people started getting up and walking off or jabbering with each other in the middle of my act. I can't fill in when somebody fall sick, step in and sing or tell jokes or dance like the rest do. I got the good sense to know that I look like a fool in a red dress and fishnet stockings, but I wear all that anyway. I can swallow anything, but that's all. So if anybody get blowed up, like as not I'll be first to go.

"Matilda," Mr. Conger say. "Get yourself up here. You're next."

One of the roustabouts got my prop trunk out by the time I get there. I stand up on that stage and look out at everybody watching me, the puddles people standing in, all them faces. And it feel like the first time, when I nearly peed myself from stage fright.

Just when Mr. Conger is about to start in on me, we hear something funny, some kind of ruckus. Mr. Conger go outside to look, and we all follow him. Way out on the edge of the field, out past the road, there's people moving. And out in front of them is something strange, tall as a tree and walking.

Mr. Conger yell for us to mind him, but then he turn around and watch the thing too.

All of us get real quiet. The walking tree come in full view and we stand there, staring. It jerk along like one of them soldiers with a toy leg in place of his real one, and it look like it soon gonna fall over. Only it don't. And behind it there's people, lots of people coming along and making all sorts of noise with their voices and horns and clapping and who know what else. The whole ruckus coming straight at us.

"What the bejesus is that?" someone say behind me.

Marie clutch my arm tight. "My land, Tildy, what do you think it could *be*?" she say all breathy in my ear.

We all stand there some more, gawking. We don't know whether to run away or run to meet the crowd. And the crowd keep coming, getting bigger and bigger, till there's so many people swarming our way, whooping and hollering, it look like two or three whole towns emptied out and joined up together.

"It's Doc Bell," I say.

All decked out in red, white, and blue satin and balancing on stilts, Doc Bell keep coming our way, pulling them people along like he got them on strings. His arms reach out and fling shiny things to the crowd and they run out and scoop them up. It's boys in short pants out there, girls with schoolbooks, clerks in collars, mothers with babes in arms, men still in their hoeing overalls. Even some bicycles and cars mixed in, honking and backfiring. Doc Bell got them all. His red and white coattails flap in the wind like flags.

"It is! My land, it's Doc Bell!" Marie squeal, and she grab my arm while she jump up and down like she mean to tear it off.

Then we get so busy talking and laughing for a minute we don't hear Mr. Conger till he's screaming at us like a maniac.

"Kidwell. *Kidwell!* Are you all deaf? Kidwell, you're on first! Carmoody and Pete, get ready to go on next! Move! Move!"

It take us a minute to get it through our heads that we gonna do a show in the middle of Thursday. We ain't never done such a thing before. It seem to strike us all at once, and we scatter like rabbits at the sound of a gun, everybody to his place.

Kidwell get his lush just right. "Lorelei" come off fine. We don't finish till it's well-nigh dark, and every one of us want to faint we're so tired. But we don't faint. Mr. Conger tell us to start all over again, and that's just what we do.

MR. CONGER catch me after the show. "Put that down," he say, and he nod at my prop trunk. So I put it down.

After Doc Bell and all the commotion, after two high-flying shows in one day, we all feeling tired but happy. But Mr. Conger don't look no more pleased than he been for weeks. The flames from the torches reflect off his eyes, and he smile some kind of nasty smile at me.

He step closer, and the flames in his eyes go out.

"I said we had new stunts for you, Matilda," he say. "You're going to do fire-eating."

I look in his face for the joke. "That ain't got nothing to do with sword-swallowing," I say back. "That's a whole nother proposition."

All you need to have to swallow a sword is a strong stomach and plenty of sand, and I got both. But you got to be crazy to swallow a burning thing. Mess up at that, and you get hurt bad.

"It'll do you good to branch out," he say.

"No, sir," I say back. "I don't want no part of that."

I reach for my prop trunk, and Mr. Conger grab my arm.

"Look here," he say. "People get tired of the same old act after a while, Matilda. People don't want to see it anymore."

"Doc Bell been playing the same towns for years," I say back to him.

"Nowadays you've got to jazz it up some, or you lose them. You lose them, Matilda."

He smile at me then, like he got me cornered. But I twist my arm away and pick up my prop trunk to go.

"It's up to you, Matilda. It's up to you how long you last."

I keep walking, but my old prop trunk feel like it got a ton of bricks in it now, and it almost make me fall. I want to just leave it there and go. Run off into the night, down them roads, away. But I can't. I got to listen to him jabbering behind me, hammering at me. I got to drag that trunk along.

NEXT DAY Marie sit in the backstage tent looking down on a map she got spread out on her lap. She sit there talking to herself like she think I ain't listening, picking places she want to go. Seem to me there ain't no rhyme nor reason to the places she favor, but I put that thought under my hat. Anyway, she know Doc Bell got a route he follow every year: start out in Florida, wend his way on up the coast through Georgia and the Carolina country, then on up through Virginia. Stop outside them little cotton or tobacco towns where they still don't know what a train or a car look like. Then slip through the corner of Maryland

and Pennsylvania and head out to Ohio for the summer. Same route every season, even when the War was on. Same little towns that seen his show every year for ten or twenty running but hardly got another thing to look forward to.

"Appafalatchie," Marie say, pointing to her map. "Doesn't that sound intriguing?"

What it sound is hard to spell, but I don't tell her so. "Could be," I say back.

She poke the map with her finger. "Missoula. That's pretty, don't you think? It sounds so *feminine* for the name of a city."

It's hard to hear her with people all around us getting ready to go on, yelling and bumping into each other. Ten or fifteen people in one little tent throwing around props and limbering up make for mighty close quarters. But Marie make herself heard.

"Mission City," she say, and sit back and smile like she just ate something good. "Can you *imagine*, Tildy?"

I got my prop trunk open to check and make sure I'm set. It's all there, knives and swords and rods, some kerchiefs in yellow and red, footstool, long coil of chain lying at the bottom like a dead snake.

She never run out of places. She never say the same one twice. I wonder if she ever think about her husband and her parlor, her warm bed and the lady friends she left behind without a word of goodbye. She never speak of any of these, and up till now, I never thought to ask.

I look down at her pretty head of curls, at her hand resting gentle on the paper she got on her lap.

"Schenectady," she say, and look up at me with eyes like rushing blue water.

When I can't find no words to answer, she say, "That's way up in New York State."

She smile. "Tildy, aren't you well? Tildy?"

That day in the mill end shop is six months old now. Six months, but it feel as warm and new as a baby born today.

"Schenectady," I say, and I'm almost whispering so she has to lean close to me to hear it. "We could find a little place there. I got some money saved. Start a shop, making frocks."

Marie lean back on her stool and put her finger back on the map.

"Perhaps," she say.

"Do some mending," I say back quiet.

"Hm."

"Start us a little garden out back."

She don't speak for a bit. Then she say, "Telluride."

I watch her hand move.

"Mountain City."

NEXT MORNING, Marie's gone when I wake up. With her out of our room, it strike me just how nasty a place this is Doc Bell got us put up in for the Midlow shows. The whole room lean down at one side, and the windows got the dirt of ages clouding them. The walls ain't even got any pictures to brighten them up. I roll over in the worn-out sheets and feel the spot where Marie slept, but it's cold now, like she was never there at all.

I can't remember a day we didn't get up together, have breakfast together. I wash up and dress in that quiet room, and it feel like she was never there beside me at all. Her things is right where she left them last night, I know. But when I pick up her shawl, then her hose, it feel like it's just cloth.

Once I got something on I step out and tiptoe down the hall and put my ear to the first door. Some of the rooms got Doc Bell's people in them and some don't, but I don't know which is which, so I listen to every one I come to. At the first one, I don't hear nothing at all. At the next one, somebody walking back and forth across the floor, over and over, and it make me uneasy to hear it. At the next door, people talking, but none of the voices is Marie.

Then I look down the hall and see one of the doors is part open. There's a slice of light coming out, and voices. And since it's just like Marie not to close a door behind herself, I walk past the rest of the closed doors to that one and peek inside.

All I can see is a little piece of room like mine, and the voices have stopped. So I push the door just a little bit, very slow. Then a little more. Still I can't see a thing but the light brightening that room. I push some more. And I hear breathing. Not normal breathing. It's heavy, like paper scraping hard over wood, and I put my hand over my bosoms just to hear such a sound. I want to leave. But I push the door a little more.

Marie step into my sight, put down her sewing basket, and step out of sight again.

I lose my breath and then get it back. I push the door a little more.

I see a lap. I see a hand resting gentle on the arm of a chair. I push, and I see Marie standing next to the freak lady. That's whose room it is. Marie step around and start fussing with the hat that cover the freak lady's head. I seen the freak lady before, going to and from her tent, wearing a red dress and that black hat with so many bows and ribbons you could almost miss how the hat's way too big for anybody's head. Nearly big around as a rain barrel. When she go by, I look away.

But I can't look away now, 'cause here is Marie, humming and chirping like a bird while she tack on a veil with a needle.

"Now that mesh might be a little hot, Miss Antoinette," Marie say, "but I think you will like how it feels."

I close my eyes. Marie go on talking, but I don't hear none of it clear in my mind.

Then I open my eyes again.

"Now you just pull the veil down when you want the sun out of your eyes. Like so. Oh my, it's stuck. Here, wait a moment."

She fuss a minute and then lift up the hat.

And I see the freak lady's head for the first time. I see what people pay to see in that tent. Terrible, but I can't take my eyes off it. It got patches of hair spread around on it, and patches that's bare as a stone. It's all swelled up like something that want to burst open. It look like it will break her neck to hold it up. But she hold her head up anyway.

Marie come over to her and touch it. At first I think she picking off a loose thread or scrap of ribbon, but she ain't. She stand close and she say, "Poor lamb," and her fingers move along as she touch different parts of the freak lady's head and watch everywhere her own fingers go.

I step back out in the hall.

I take a few more steps, then I run. Back to my own room. Feel like my whole stomach coming right up my throat, but when I get to the washbasin, it's only dry heaves. Ain't nothing left to come out of me at all.

THE LAST night we play Midlow, a little wind kick up and make the big tent shimmy, but not too bad. Crowd ain't as big as the day Doc Bell pulled in folks from miles around, but plenty of folks come out to see us.

When I come on, Mr. Conger tip his bowler to the crowd and flash a big smile and start up his patter, and I bow and open up my prop trunk.

"Now, ladies and gentlemen, watch closely, you won't see anything like this again, watch closely, that's an ice pick she's holding, ladies and gentlemen, the *genuine* article."

I step out in my red dress and fishnets and hold up the ice pick while Mr. Conger go jabbering on, and I try to look at the little children out there to keep my mind clear of Marie and the freak lady.

"There is no trick here, ladies and gentlemen, I assure you. Please keep your seats and hold your applause until Matilda the Great has safely withdrawn the ice pick."

I keep my throat straight and slide it down till the handle hit my teeth, then I pull it out real slow. Then I kneel down and stick it in some corkboard so they see it got a point just like the one they got at home. When I stand up, a few people clap a bit.

"Now, ladies and gentlemen, your attention please as Matilda the Great attempts to ingest a genuine Union and Pacific regulation railroad spike. That's *solid Indiana pig iron*, ladies and gents."

I kneel down again and strike the spike against the handle of my prop trunk so it ring like a bell, and somehow it fall out my hand on the stage. I look at Mr. Conger and he look at me. I don't never drop a thing. His mouth make the words, *Pick it up.*

Then he say to the audience, "Quiet, please. Everyone, Matilda the Great must have silence."

When I look out there, Marie standing way back in the center aisle. She look at me and then she look out across the field to the road. All the while, out the corner of my eye, I see Mr. Conger trying to get my attention to get me to stand up and carry on with the act. But I wait there on my knee until Marie get around to looking at me again.

I hold out a hand and say, "I need my assistant. Come on up here."

She make a little *Who, me?* kind of gesture, and then she smile and shake her head. Then she look around at the people looking at her, and smile again, and walk toward me. Her eyes are big and bright, and she clutch up the skirts of her white frock to keep from tripping while she walk, then run, up the aisle. And I wait for her.

When Marie take my hand and I pull her up on the stage, I know I ain't Matilda the Great no more. I know we got to take a new name now. Maybe we will be the Missoula Sisters. Maybe we will be the Schenectady Girls.

I will let Marie pick a name she like. I think about that and the cold metal spike going down inside me, stretching out my throat, coming to rest. I will let go, and it will stay right where I put it, just like it always do. But soon enough, it won't be just cold metal I put in me every night. It will be fire, too.

A Night in Vienna

Felix Conger

———

SUN'S COMING UP, we've been traveling all night, and Doc Bell ain't hearing a word I say about stopping a bit to rest his troupers. Course it's me who'll have to smooth feathers all day. Ain't it my job to keep everything rosy? Calm folks down even though they'll have to work without a wink of decent sleep? Head off a revolt when the pay's late again? Sure, Felix'll be on top of it! Keep the torches from sending us up in flames 'cause Doc won't switch over to electric lights? Turn a profit with a wagonload of broken-down has-beens who think cake-walking and buck dancing are all the rage these days? Go ahead, Felix. Make the payroll when we can't draw enough rubes these days to fill up a decent quilting bee? Carry just as many acts as Barnum himself, like it's still Doc's gravy days? Leave it to Felix, all right. Never mind that the few rubes we do pull in are so stingy they won't part with so much as a nickel most nights.

 When we crossed over from Maryland, Doc says to me, "Think I'll spend me awhile here, Felix," as if he just found the Promised

Land. "Pennsylvania?" I say. "Why hang around in a place full of prissy-britches Quakers?" Doc just winked.

So here we are, stalled in Pennsylvania when we should've been in Ohio long ago. All summer, Doc's been playing it close to the vest, not saying what's on his mind. And this morning's no different. He sits there swiveling his big head, sweeping his eyes over the scene, taking it all in and making his plans. Out of the blue he points to a spot and tells me to pull over. "Land lay just perfect for us there," he says. "We gonna be snug as a tick in a floozy's bosoms."

He hops out of the car and stretches his mile-long legs. When I get out, it feels like I'm standing in quicksand. The trucks and the cars sink halfway to the axles. We might as well try setting up the show in a bucket of shaving cream. We're gonna have to haul rocks to steady the stage. Lay down some boards to keep the rubes from drowning in mud before they get to their seats. Extra stakes and lines for all the tents. Drainage ditches. Ventilation. Bugs. It'll be ten times the work setup should be, and I can hear the kvetching already. It'll take every minute we've got between now and tomorrow night to get ready.

Doc looks my way and smiles. And boy, don't I know what's coming.

"Think I'll give the lads and lasses the morning off," he says.

Sure, I could argue. But I might as well spit at the sun.

ME, I'M ON the job. I've got to find the owner and strike a deal for the use of the land. Get the surrounding towns billed so the rubes know there's a show to go see. Find somewhere to put the troupers up for the night, and that ain't easy with the blacks. Sniff around till I know who to bribe to keep the local authorities from busting up the show to protect their innocent women and children from our evil influence. There're no mornings off for Felix Conger.

There ain't a soul out on the roads, just me and the pigs and the cows in the fields. After a while the lonely road puts me in mind of that other road, the one where we lost Haines a month back. That's how it comes to me: lost him. Like a copper penny that slipped through a hole in your pocket out in a hayfield. Like you might look up one day and there he'd be, all in one piece, that guitar he never would've left behind on purpose slung over his shoulder again.

Even in daylight every road out here looks like every other one. Night Haines and the others didn't show up, it took us hours to find the car and to track down the rest of them on a farm nearby. I must've asked Lily a hundred times, *Why?* Why didn't you all stay together? Why let him go wandering off by himself on some overgrown, pitch-black cow path in the middle of nowhere?

And what'd she say? Haines ain't her problem!

Fleet got between us and walked me away, cooled me down. It's not really blood I want anyway, it's a deal. Take any of the rest of them. Take Lily, Rafer, any of that crew of loafers. Take that crazy Svetlana—I can teach anyone to be a medium in a week. Or take the freak, worst of the lot. I begged Doc, *begged* him not to bring her on board. Told him it'd pull the whole show down, vile thing like that. Or all of them. Take all of them, just give me back Haines.

He could play a guitar like nobody I'd heard before. You'd listen to him and you'd think, yeah, sure, I know that one. Heard it a million times before, know it inside out and upside down, could whistle it in my sleep. Like it fine, though it ain't one of my favorites. Only by the time he's done with it, it is. A damned good song, you're thinking. Reminds you of the first girl you kissed, or your best night with your buddies, or your mama laying you down in your cradle after she'd sung you to sleep. And how the hell would you remember that? He made you, that's how.

Only Doc wasn't interested. Haines couldn't do any tricks, couldn't dance at all, couldn't get off a joke to save his life. We almost left him down there in Apopka, Florida, where I found him while Doc was wintering. Wasn't till the day we're pulling out he says, "Felix, your heart telling you take this boy on?" It was funny, not how I'd have put it, but I said, "Yeah, sure, Doc."

There was nothing he couldn't play. Rags and reels, ballads and blues. I played him a couple of Schubert lieder on the piano and he picked them up on one listen. I got him record albums. I snuck him into my room and left him there for hours, listening, soaking it up till he could play it all. And not one bit of it did Doc want in the show.

A horn blares, and a big, topless touring car comes right at me. I swerve to the right just in time, but I land half in the mud. After that, I'm just spinning my wheels, stuck in a slough.

I get out and have a look around. Nothing but cornfields, hay-fields, a fallow field, a few trees, a couple of goddamned cow ponds. I put on my bowler and get ready for a walk. Maybe it'll clear my head. I keep having spells like this, waking up like I've been sleeping in the middle of the day. I walk down the road a bit, change my mind, come back. There's something else I ought to do. I open the trunk and take out a sack.

At the bottom of the hill there's a pond, hardly bigger than a puddle. I stop at the edge, squat down in the reeds, and open the sack. It fell to me to keep his records. Old darkie like Fleet wouldn't know any better than to eat his dinner off them, and that wife of his I wouldn't let touch them. I take out the first one, turn it over, toss it in the water. It spins a bit, floats for a second and goes down. When I was a boy, sitting *shivah* for one of the old people, I wondered why'd I have to act like a dead person to mourn the dead. It made me crazy, sitting around for so long, never going out, never changing my clothes, never even paring my fingernails. I take out another black disk with its gray label, its fancy white lettering, and I throw that one in, too. And the next. Just a little while's all it takes, and I'm finished.

It has to be done. I'm sorry for what happened to him, but I don't want Haines haunting me. In my line of work, you can't have every godforsaken piece of country road turning you into some mooning idiot. You've got to be sharp. You've got to stay one step ahead of the troupers and the rubes, both. You've got to be on your game.

Then I remember the guitar, still in the trunk. I ought to get it and weigh it down with some stones, throw it in, too. Finish the job. Half a burial's got to be worse than none at all.

FIRST NIGHT of the show, everything looks fine. Stage and tents in place, pretty good crowd settling in. And I've got us square with the local potentates. It should be a decent night.

My last stop's the one I've been avoiding. The freak show tent. Over the years Doc and I've run every kind of act you can think of, from snake charmers to séances, but never a thing like this. "It's a clean show you've got, Doc," I told him. "You're pulling in whole families, the civic ladies, the church deacons. You can't have something worse than a coochie show dragging down your reputation." But Doc says it'll be clean. Says the rubes'll love it, wait and see.

Lily's out front at the ticket stand, smoking. I slip in for a quick check, and the sound of that breathing stops me cold. Like some fish that climbed out of a swamp, that sound. Enough to make your skin crawl right off your body. I try to keep my eyes off that flickering lamplight in the corner, the screen, the shadows, the whole shtick that Doc cooked up, but it gets me. I can't go another step.

Only by circling around the back of her can I make myself go closer. The ragged breathing makes me want to plug up my ears. You can't even hear the rest of the show in here. You wouldn't know there was one. Just this. Just this thing that started out a woman, that would be better off dead.

I ain't got the stomach for it today. So I go back out without checking anything, even the props, and march over to the other side tent, Madame Svetlana's. The old witch is inside, in all her gypsy beads and bracelets, sitting back in a corner behind a little table like she's waiting for tea service from the maid. She frowns when she sees me.

"Are you blind?" I say.

"What?" she squawks. "What do you want?"

"It's sopping wet in here," I say. "You giving fishing lessons? No? Then go get something to soak up the puddles. And where're your props? Where're the crystal ball and the pictures that're supposed to be on the walls?"

For this I get a stare.

"What is this, a sanatorium? Jump to it! C'mon!"

She slithers out of her chair and huffs past me.

Now that I've got my blood flowing right again, I straighten up. Breathe a little easier. Snap my thumbs up and down under my lapels, because me, I've got to look flush no matter what shape the books are in. And it's almost time for the show.

WE'RE WELL under way, playing to a respectable crowd, when Lily finds me in the backstage tent.

"What?" I say. "I'm busy."

"She's gone."

"Gone? Who's gone?"

"Sheba."

She turns and walks out.

I chase her out behind the tent. "Wait a minute! What the hell do you mean, she's gone? Gone where?"

Lily shrugs. "Said she's too sick for the tent tonight."

By the time we get back there, a throng is threatening to pull the tent down. Some of the rubes're yelling about the good money they paid for nothing, others keep trying to push up closer to see what all the fuss is about, and the rest're simmering toward a boil for the fun of it. We're far enough from the stage that it's not interrupting the show yet, but it will soon enough at this rate.

I get myself up on the ticket stand fast as a hiccough. Wave my arms, jump up and down, holler about giving every ticket holder a free gift and everyone waiting a free ticket for tomorrow. It takes a few minutes, but I finally get them calmed down and set Lily to handing out the tickets. That'll keep them quiet till I can grab some of Doc's tchotchkes to hand out. It'll cost us some, but it's better than a brawl.

Fannie's on by the time I'm done. Pistols aren't what I want to see right now, to tell you the truth, but it goes off fine. She's on a roll, in fact. Got the crowd hanging on every trick, cheering all the stunts like she's picking thimbles off a fence a mile away with spitballs.

I should go grab a bucket of whistles or hatpins to hand out to the ticket holders back at Sheba's tent, but they can wait. I go find Doc instead.

He's in the back of a motor truck putting on his Pilgrim costume. Cocks one eyebrow and gives me a look that says, Why are you bothering me with the details, Felix Conger? Didn't I hire you to handle those?

"You got the crowd settled down?" he asks when I'm done, picking up his big black hat with its white band.

"That Sheba bit's got to go," I say.

"You don't say."

"I mean it, Doc. We're in over our heads. No telling what troubles it'll cause next time. We've got to get rid of it."

Doc smiles. "Little tussle ain't gonna sink us, Felix. We seen a few before."

Doc's famous for them, in fact. Fistfights, melees, even a lynch mob. I've heard all the stories and some I've lived through myself, including a few fool-headed stunts Doc himself pulled over the years. There ain't been a mess yet Doc hasn't come through fine, and we both goddamned know it.

"It's filth," I say. "Nothing but filth."

Doc gives me a slow once-over glance.

"Felix, we ain't selling Liberty Bonds. This here's the med show biz, son. That gal's taking in plenty of money, and I ain't about to drop her." He looks at me hard and then starts buttoning on his square, white collar. "You ain't been yourself lately, not since that boy went missing. Maybe you oughta take a little break."

It's twelve years now I've been with Doc Bell. Ain't one day of one season I've missed, not the whole time. I can't believe my ears.

Doc grabs his Bible and his lamp, slides past me, and heads for the stage. I get out and watch him stride through the dark, the light swinging beside him. I watch Ma Fleet bow and slip offstage, and then Doc Bell steps out onstage and puts out the torches and says, "Now every one of you here tonight know the story about how the world began in *darkness*."

And I think to myself, what does he know about darkness? In a little while, he'll come out carrying the pillowcase that's supposed to be a tapeworm. But has he ever even seen a tapeworm? If one thrashed in his gut, poked its head out his ass, slithered in a glop of slimy shit down the inside of his pants leg and sat there at his feet in a pool of corruption, would Doc Bell even know what he was looking at?

Then I get my wits back and get to work.

NEXT MORNING, I wake up late again. And I mean late. Seems I can't get enough sleep these days, and this morning's even worse. Feels like somebody slipped in my room in the night and glued me to the sheets. I look at my watch and it's way past noon.

I'm pulling on my trousers when some paper flutters out of my pocket. It's an envelope, belonged to Haines. Fleet gave it to me, said it was set up to go to Haines's mama. Amelia Haines in Apopka, it's addressed to. No letter inside, though. Never was, Fleet said. Probably a lie. Shifty, shuffling way he said it told me right off he didn't want the boy's letter to his mama touching Felix Conger's hands.

I'm good enough to write to her, though, tell her about it and how sorry Doc Bell and the troupers are for her loss. Thing is, I ain't done it yet. Keep meaning to, and another day passes without me getting the job done. Now it's been weeks, and this morning's all of a sudden the one I can't let another day pass. There's a little table by the window. I've got no paper, though. I rifle the drawers, ransack the closet, toss my trunk. Nothing.

And just what am I going to say to Amelia Haines in Apopka anyway? Ma'am, your son played a guitar beautifully. Did she know? Will it make it better or worse when I speak of all that promise that'll never blossom? And oh, yes, by the way, ma'am, it was one of Doc Bell's own troupers that got your son in whatever trouble he found that night he disappeared. Old sow didn't want him around. That'll sure be a consolation to his mother. And here's something else you should know about your son, Amelia Haines. Doc was about to have me pull him off the stage anyway. Knock him down to roustabout, see how long he lasted. For this we took him from you. For this I lured your son out of Florida, ma'am, and from the looks of it, he'll never come home to you again. And how should I close such a letter? Peace be with you, Amelia Haines, if any peace you can find.

I get up and put on my suit jacket and tuck a pink handkerchief in my breast pocket. Then I lie down on the bed again. I don't mean to go to sleep, but I do. And when I wake up a second time, it's sundown and the show's starting without me.

WHEN I GET to the showgrounds, they're on the third act. Carmoody and Pete are up, doing the Risley act, Carmoody on his back tumbling Pete in the air with his feet. I slip into the crowd, mix in with some locals, drift back to the empty seats, sit on one of the benches. Nobody pays me any mind. I watch Kidwell limping around the stage in our country doctor skit. Then Fannie comes out and sings the Gold Rush song, sashays her way through that little dance with the pickaxe that gets the fellas in the first rows hot and bothered. How many millions of times have I seen all of this, how many millions more have I heard it from the backstage tent? I know every line and every step, but I watch anyway just like everybody around me. Then there's a juggling bit, Carmoody and Pete slinging potatoes and cabbages and a ham through the air, and it's snappier than I've seen it come off in quite a while. Maybe all those changes I've been making are finally working out. After a while I forget the order on the bill for tonight. Laugh and clap right along with the locals. Marie brings out Matilda the Great and talks up the stunts so well they get the audience oohing and aaahing and holding their breath right away. It's a good night, looks like, and I'm glad I came. I'm feeling pretty good, in fact, for the first time in a while.

And I think what a kick he'd get out of the show, my father. Those nights years ago in Yonkers come back to me, waking up when he shook my shoulder, following tiptoe out of the house so my mother wouldn't hear. Downtown we'd go, to the hotels or the waterfront. And my father sang right there under the stars as the people strolled by, stopping to listen now and then. His tenor rising into the night sky, arias, German lieder, songs of cruel beauty and death for love. I opened my violin case and set it up so the people walking by could pitch in coins. Or we went to his favorite place, the sidewalk outside the city orphanage after the gaslights were on. The children opened the windows and leaned out, laughing and clapping.

Between songs, in quiet moments, he whispered to me. "When we go to Vienna, Felix, you'll eat so much strudel your fingers will stick to your strings." It was something different, some new treat, every time he mentioned Vienna. Eventually we'd go home. Still in the dark. To save face for the family, he only went out by night. Six months after he gave in to them and took a respectable job driving one of the fish trucks, he was dead. That's when they stopped calling him crazy, *meshuggeh*, a shame on them all, a husband and father wandering the streets, singing for pennies like a gypsy.

I look up on the stage, and there's Doc Bell. He's dressed in his Uncle Sam suit, white top hat, striped pants, the whole nine yards.

"Mothers, are your children sickly?" he asks. "Do they tire out easy when the other children still have the vim and vigor to play?"

He steps closer to the audience.

"My friends, the secret to vitality is very simple. It is not medicinal herbs and tonics. It is not pills and powders and potions. Nothing can make a body act like Nature intended except Nature herself. That's the God's honest truth."

It gets quiet.

"A body needs rest. That's how Nature restores us, brothers and sisters. When we rest. And any disturbance that robs a body of rest has to be stopped. Is there a mother out there whose child has a cough?"

Three or four women stand up. Lots more squirm like they want to. Doc goes on and tells them how deadly a cough is, how it saps the heart, the brain, the blood. How his formula brings rest and relief. He asks for a child to come up on the stage and try some for free.

A woman pushes up and heaves a boy on the stage. And even from where I'm sitting, I can see the child's condition. Looks about eight, gaunt white face, arms like sticks. I don't know what he's got, but he needs way more than Doc's VIM-TANA to keep him from wasting away to nothing.

Doc gets down on one knee. "What's your name, son?" he says.

I get up and push out of the row where I'm sitting. Doesn't he see how bad off the boy is?

The boy says something in a feeble voice.

On Doc goes, even though it's his rule not to. He won't sell to anybody as sick as the boy. I push up toward the front of the crowd, till finally he sees me. For one second he looks at me, and I think, this is it, he'll stop.

He turns back. "Erasmus, son, how old are you?" he says.

"Ten, sir."

Doc claps his hand on the boy's shoulder. And I back away. Out of the range of the torchlight. Away from the stage. Far enough so I can't hear what's going on up there anymore, and then farther, till I'm lost among the people milling around the showgrounds. Some of them look at me funny. What's it they see? I look down at myself, pat my clothes. Then I remember, some've been here before, seen me onstage. I walk on, lose myself among them again. It's a clear night, no rain, good air. I overhear talk of berry pies, escaped pigs, leaks in the roof, rats in the cellar. I keep moving, brushing shoulders, wisps of hair, trails of breath all around me in the dark.

And just like that I'm at the freak show tent. With Doc Bell on, there're no rubes about. The torches are down to flickers. That slob, Lily, looks at me from her ticket stand, smoking a cigarette down so far her fingers look empty.

She spits out a butt and hops down off her stand. Before I know what she's doing, she's grabbing at me.

"That all you got?" she says, holding up a length of twine.

I hadn't even realized I had it.

She pushes the stand up close to the tent and climbs on top of it and starts tying up one of the banners that's hanging loose across the front. But I can hardly see her anymore. I'm looking down, feeling the way the twine slid off my fingers where I'd looped it around them. Both hands. I look at the flap of the tent, at that one, thin drape of canvas between me and the miserable wretch inside.

"Hey! You got any more string?" Lily yells somewhere above me.

They're shaking. The same hands that used to practice for hours and hours, until my fingers blistered and swelled, just to accompany my father those nights outside the orphanage. He would stop me and hold them in his own hands and say that they deserved rest, that if I treated them well they would one day play the violin so it sang even more beautifully than any voice ever could. And what would he say to me if he saw me now? What would he think of me? *Ah, Felix, how could this be? Did you forget what the music is for?*

Somehow I get away. I stumble out into the field. Among the show cars, I find the two-seater Doc and I use, but I can't touch it. I start walking instead, I don't even know what direction. And I keep going till the sun comes out again.

❧ ❧

A ROUGH hand on my shoulder wakes me up. I pick my head up off the bar. It's a policeman, one of Chicago's finest, fat Irish cop with muttonchop whiskers and squinty eyes, looking at me like he's gonna kick me down the sewer. And me, well, I ain't resisting.

"Officcr," I say, only it comes out more like "Fsssssshhhhrr."

The cop looks around at all the guilty fellas in the joint, little saloon over on the South Side. Whiskey everywhere, we're all guilty of violating the prohibition. Most're bar birds just like me, in here every day dropping what little money we've got on whatever the barkeep's got to sell. Bathtub gin, corn whiskey that'd make you go bald, beer that tastes like soapwater. Damned war prohibition makes it tough being a rummy, specially when there ain't no war anymore.

"Now, would you be the Yid this belongs to?" the cop says.

He holds up Haines's guitar. Stupid me, I turn around and look where I left it to see if it's really gone. Nearly throws me off the stool, doing it. But I see it ain't where I left it.

"Yessir, fsssshhhr," I say. "That's me."

"What's your name?"

"Felix David Conger."

He gives me a long, hard look like he's thinking. Then he takes the other arm from behind his back and it's got a kid at the end. Snot-

99

nosed scamp with a face full of freckles, ten or eleven at best, cap big as a bucket sliding off his head. Hand-me-down clothes from the looks of them and shoes tied with string to hold 'em together.

"You know this rat?"

The kid takes an interest in the floor, but I ain't seen him before, and I say so.

"Witness says he took the thing from you."

Now I get it. Kid's a thief, took me for an easy mark. Not like I should care, but I try to catch the kid's eye. He ain't looking my way for anything, though.

"Hey, you," I say to the kid. "Pick that up."

He does.

"Let me hear you play."

He looks at it like he doesn't know what it is. Then he clutches the neck and strums it. A few awkward chords, enough to make you stuff your ears with cotton. But this ain't the first time he's had one in his hands, I can tell.

"Now I remember," I say to the cop. "Student of mine. Ain't any good, but he pays for my time."

The cop grunts, lets go of the kid, wipes his hands together like he just touched offal, and marches out of the place without disturbing another person.

The kid stands there like a wax dummy after the cop's long gone. My glass is empty. Dry, in fact. I pick it up and tap him on the forehead with it, and he looks up at me at last.

"Get out of here," I say, "before I make you buy me another drink. And you be back at nine tomorrow morning, hear? Lucky for you I've got a few years of free time I ain't figured out how to fill yet." I wink at him. "You've got a lot to learn."

Our Lady of the Looms

Marie Davenport

———

MY PHOTOGRAPH in last week's local newspaper, the *News and Tribune*, is so delightful that I have to sneak a look and read the small article again:

> Miss Marie Davenport of Doc Bell's Miracles and Mirth Medicine Show arrived in town yesterday. A rambunctious filly with a sparkling sense of humor and a warm heart, she invites everyone to see her live stage performance of breathtaking magic and daring stunts. Never one to miss an opportunity for fun, she kept this reporter in stitches for the better part of an hour. Truly a marvel of feminine beauty and worldly grace, Miss Davenport will be in town with the show for an additional week. Do not miss her!

"Isn't it wonderful?" I ask Tildy when she wakes up.

She pushes it away, groans, and rolls over as if I have asked her to break rocks with a pickaxe all day.

"Pshaw," I say, and get up and place the copy on top of the pile of copies I purchased. "You're simply jealous."

I've already apologized for the way the article omits any mention of her. "What choice did I have? Nobody will come flocking to see me if I say I'm just your assistant!"

But Tildy only sits on her side of the bed staring at the floor, lost in yet another of her black moods.

The summer has been difficult for her, I know. First, trying and failing to master the new fire-eating stunts Mr. Conger wanted her to learn. Had Doc Bell himself not put an end to her dogged efforts, Tildy might well have gone up in flames. Then the loss of her pay, which Doc Bell has withheld from the entire troupe for these last several weeks as he attempted to get the show back on solid footing. The disappearance of the young guitar player, Mr. Haines, saddened us all. And of course it shocked us to hear that Mr. Conger had deserted us! Without those two and other departed souls, we have surely lost some of our oomph. But Doc Bell assures us that as a smaller and more nimble ensemble, we will be back in good form that much sooner, and I believe he will prove to be right. We need only stay firm and buck up our spirits.

I open our door and sniff for a whiff of breakfast. There seems to be food in the offing if we will only get ourselves downstairs to eat it. When I close the door, Tildy still hasn't moved.

"Tildy, must you be so glum?" I ask her.

Truly, I don't see the use of it. Yet she sits there as if she will mope away the entire morning in her night frock, making us miss breakfast in the process. She doesn't even answer me, so far down in the doldrums has she sunk.

So I creep up behind her and slip my fingers under her arms. A little poking and prodding is all it takes to draw frantic snorts and giggles from her, and suddenly she is as lively as a pony in a field of clover. "Marie!" she shrieks, kicking and thrashing in an effort to get loose. But I only scoot my fingers down her sides and scuttle them over her stomach. She falls back against me, helpless, sparkles of bright laughter pouring out of her, filling the room. I doubt anyone but me ever hears that delightful sound! Then, knowing that I will make her pee herself if I don't soon stop, I let her go and dash to the opposite corner of the room, out of her reach.

She sits up and clamps one hand over her bosoms as if she is suffering heart failure. From the look on her face, you would think she was not entirely sure what just happened to her.

"You trying to kill me?" she gasps. "I'm too old for that nonsense!"

But she can't help smiling now, and both of us giggle. She looks down at her night frock, twisted around her like a pile of rags, and we laugh again.

"Look at me!" she says.

"Oh, heavens," I say dramatically. "I'm so very, very sorry to have mussed up your fine, fine garments. Perhaps Madame will consent to have me send off to Paris for a new frock—"

Before I can get to the end of my sentence, we are falling all over ourselves giggling again.

Just then there's a knock. The door, which I must have neglected to lock again, opens up. The owner sticks in his burr of a head, looks around at the both of us as if we are livestock on display in a barn, and asks us if we want breakfast.

I'll never understand why Tildy is so bashful. She goes onstage half-dressed every night! Still, she gasps and turns away from him.

"Yes, we would like breakfast this morning," I say for the both of us.

"Best be getting down 'fore it all go, then," he says unhelpfully, and then, unable to think of a way to vex us further, I suppose, he finally closes the door.

"My land," I say, crossing the room to lock the door. "He leaves something to be desired as a host, wouldn't you say?"

But Tildy is as dour as ever again, stuffing herself hastily into her clothes as if she has suddenly found herself naked in the middle of Trafalgar Square.

DESPITE HER demeanor these days, Tildy and I have settled into an understanding that is beneficial to us both. Much to my relief, it has put an end to the tensions between us and restored a most harmonious equilibrium. And now, once again, I am free to amuse myself among the endless fascinations of the members of Doc Bell's show, who never fail to be as entertaining offstage as they are on.

Mr. Haines was perhaps my favorite. In addition to providing the occasional music lesson, he gave in to my begging and pleading and allowed me to accompany him on one of the mysterious late-night excursions he undertook from time to time. His object, I discovered, was what he charmingly called "home brew." We set off on an odyssey across the countryside, like a pair of banditos in search of loot! After our first adventure, I became his regular sidekick. There was no nook or cranny too inaccessible, no hidden valley or hollow too dark and remote, for Mr. Haines's and my visits. The wily bootleggers evaded the authorities by setting up their stills in caves, under overturned wagons, in rabbit hutches, even in abandoned wells. And though Mr. Haines and I drew more than a few stares from these country bumpkins, unlikely companions that we seemed, we never failed to find and secure our goal.

While Mr. Haines and I were forced by circumstances to pass the occasional night together, most often I returned to Tildy long before daybreak. And so it was with all of my adventures, innocent in almost every case, each and every one of them. And yet, no amount of reassurance, no cajoling and sweet talk, no tender kisses nor loving touches, nothing this side of the hereafter, would ever satisfy Tildy, poor lamb, that she and she alone was the object of my truest love.

Perhaps it was the day she called me up to the stage that changed her mind and heart. Since then we have been inextricably bound, sisters treading the boards together to bring delight to the farmers and small townsfolk who come to see our shows. And what a natural I have proven to be! More than once I have reminded Tildy that fortune smiled upon her when she allied herself with a partner who could talk rings around the devil himself. Mr. Conger's departure has been a tremendous loss to us all, but my flair and elocution have made Tildy's feats of derring-do even more exciting, if the rapt attention and hearty applause from the audience may be taken as a guide.

And as well, Mr. Fleet says I am coming along nicely with the song and dance numbers I have taken it upon myself to learn. Though I am the first to admit that I have two left feet, he has patiently and with good humor led me through rehearsal after rehearsal, until my progress led him to remark that I show quite a bit of promise. And though mine was never the finest of the voices gathered round the parlor piano, Mr. Fleet says that I more than make up for it in spunk. So comfortable am I before an audience now that I am coming to feel those songs are truly my mother tongue, revealed to me only now that I have found my calling.

I am happy. Not in many years have I been so happy. So it is quite a shock when I look up toward the end of my performance of "Dear Old Dad" and catch a glimpse of a face, shadowy but familiar, in the forward rows of the audience.

My husband, John Hartford Davenport III, has found me!

THAT EVENING, after the show, we ride back to our rooms in one of the motor trucks. Once Tildy has helped me up, we sit side by side, shoulder to shoulder, in pitch darkness I would once have been loath to endure. She takes my hand for comfort, as I knew she would.

But my distress cannot be so easily relieved. I could not tell whether my husband knew I had seen him, but it is safe to assume that he did, since little escaped a man such as him. In all the eleven years of our marriage, John had not once forgotten my birthday, and he never failed to celebrate the day with some rare and exquisite bauble nestled in a jeweled box in a bed of silk paisley or black velvet. Nor had he neglected a single anniversary, which annually occasioned a visit by us to New York, San Francisco, Paris, Rome, or some other grand destination. If I came to the breakfast table a bit distracted, by noon a delivery boy arrived at the door bearing Belgian chocolates or Brazilian orchids. And never was he jealous of time I spent with friends near and far, even when I vanished for days at a time. Silly cuckoo-bird, he would call me when he arrived home at the end of his long day, tired by the demands of seeing to it that all of his factories hummed with industry morning, noon, and night. My silly cuckoo-bird must have what she desires.

I feel Tildy shift herself in the darkness and breathe into my ear.

"Things go okay tonight?" she asks.

"Just fine," I reply, "though perhaps I lacked a bit of my usual pep. How did you think I was this evening? Hard as I try with that first bit, I just can't seem to get the Italian accent exactly right."

Far be it from Tildy to offer an enthusiastic reaction. "Sounded all right to me," she says.

"'All right?' Well, heavens," I say. "Then I can't imagine why I didn't get called out for sixteen encores."

Somebody with a bit more appreciation chuckles in the dark. How strange to travel this way, in the midst of friendly faces that you cannot see at all.

"Folks liked your song," Tildy says, referring to the new number we tried tonight. "Singing seem to get you all kind of attention."

For a moment I'm at a loss for words. Does she know?

"Well, ah—" I stammer. "I've put a great deal of work into it. It's gratifying that the effort is finally paying off."

106

I turn around and look at her in the dark, but I can see only the dimmest outline, the faintest glow from the white shirtwaist she wears over her sequined costume. I'm starting to feel a little uncomfortable being unable to see, but I am certain she is referring to that silly newspaper article. You would think the thing was a declaration of war, the way it annoys her. And then it comes to me. John must have seen it. Somehow the tiny, local Pennsylvania ragsheet fell into his hands, and that is how he tracked me down. How foolish I was! Such is his network of friends and associates, that the most obscure corner of a thoroughly backward region affords me no refuge at all.

Tildy's and my chatter drops off into silence. She holds my hand for the entirety of the ride and only lets go when she's helped me down from the bed of the motor truck.

Back in our room, I look around and imagine what John would think of such squalor. The bedraggled, dirty linens dripping off the bed, the dim and sooty walls, the lack of any ornament that might bring a touch of gladness to the place. It is funny what one can become accustomed to over time, until one sees only what one chooses to regard.

Once my eyes have traveled the circuit of the distasteful room, I find Tildy staring at me with that hangdog look of hers.

"Tildy, have you no manners whatever?" I ask, turning away and reaching behind to unfasten my skirt. "I am not an exhibit at the Science Pavilion of the Chicago Exposition. Get yourself ready for bed."

I fumble with the clasp, unable to open the accursed thing. She walks over and undoes it for me. Usually it is I who must initiate our every tryst, she who pleads fatigue or distraction half of the time, but this evening she surprises me. I feel her hands linger at my waist. Then she does something most peculiar. From behind she encircles me with her arms, traps me for a moment so that I cannot raise my own, and presses her cheek into my hair. Then she releases me and walks away.

I turn around and smile. "If that is what passes for affection where you hail from," I say teasingly, "I will have to provide some further instruction."

She doesn't smile.

"Tildy!" I say, and stamp my foot. "You are infuriating!"

She crosses her arms. "How long was you planning to stay?" she asks.

"Stay?" I ask. "Stay where? Tildy, what do you—"

And then I understand. She must have seen John as well. She must have recognized him from the mill end shop, even after all this time, after so many miles. What on earth was so memorable in that bland face of his that it remained with her all this time? I can scarcely believe my ears.

"You wasn't going to say a thing about him," she says.

"What cause was there? Now that he knows where I have gone, he will return to his affairs."

"No, he won't."

"How in heaven's name would you know?"

For a moment I think she will answer me, then she turns away and goes to the dresser where a pitcher and basin sit. She pours water sloppily into the basin and splashes her face with it. Then, to my astonishment, she bends over and plunges her face right in the stale water.

I feel I am drowning just looking at her, but she remains there. I rush over and pull her back, and we stagger and nearly fall from the motion.

"Tildy, what is the *matter* with you?" I demand, but she only turns away and buries her face in a cloth.

Her shoulders shake, but not a sound escapes her. I lead her over to the bed and sit her down. She will not take the cloth away from her face, so I press myself close to her and take her in my arms and tell her.

"Never in a million years," I say, "would I abandon you to return to my husband."

AND YET. And yet, when I step onstage the next night under a lovely canopy of stars, John is there again. He sits in just the same spot, and this time he has brought one of his lackeys with him.

By late in the evening I am so nervous I barely make it through my last turn onstage. When I come off, Mr. Fleet, bless his heart, takes one look at me and asks me what is the matter.

I tell him about John. He peeks out the backstage curtain, sees the two of them sitting there, and ducks out the back entrance. I can't imagine what he might be doing, but it makes me feel better.

I go and seat myself beside Tildy, expecting her to tell me not to worry, but she doesn't say anything to me. She just sits in front of her little mirror, wiping off her makeup.

I wonder what he will do. How many times will he come to the show and sit in front of me in the manner of a hunter tracking his prey? How many times will I make it through my performances before the sight of him unsettles me so badly that I forget my lines or miss a step? Will he stand up while I am onstage, point a finger at me, and denounce me for a fraud?

After the show, as I am approaching one of the trucks, his voice comes to me from behind a tree just off the road.

"Marie."

John shows himself, a shadow beside the trunk. In all of the bustle, nobody has heard those melancholy tones but me.

"Marie, please. Give me a moment."

What am I to do? I can't ignore my own husband! I glance around, see I am unobserved, and walk out to where he is standing.

I expect, at the least, recriminations. My land, I abandoned the man without so much as a note of goodbye! But he makes none whatsoever. For several moments we simply stand wordless in the shelter of a copse of trees, and the only sound is the hubbub of the show closing down behind us. I cannot see him clearly, but he appears haggard, more gaunt than when I last saw him.

"It's been terrible without you," he says, his voice breaking. "I dreaded so much to return to that house that I sold it."

"Good heavens!" I say, astonished, knowing how he loved that house. "Surely you—"

"If it meant nothing to you, it is worthless to me," he says. "You must come home with me."

He says it so simply, without bitterness, that I know I am forgiven. How kind a man he is capable of being.

"Why this, Marie? You know that I'll give you anything you want. You needn't wallow in this carnival debauchery—" He stops, fearing, perhaps, that he has overstepped some boundary. "Marie, think of your welfare, as I do. Please."

"I am fine, John," I say to reassure him, but it is as if he hasn't heard me.

We walk in silence a while longer.

"I am so very sorry," I say.

He takes my hand. "Think overnight, Marie. I'll return tomorrow."

Before I can speak, he steps back, fades into shadows, and disappears into the trees.

I find Tildy waiting for me when I return to the truck, her arms crossed, silent as an Indian totem. The truck rumbles into gear, the back gate drops, and a hand reaches out of the dark interior to help us aboard.

"After you," Tildy says.

IN THE MIDDLE of the night, she nudges me and doggedly begins an interrogation.

"Tildy, please, I am exhausted," I plead.

"What did you say to him?" she asks.

I sigh and rub my tired eyes. What am I to say now? How can I answer without disturbing her even further?

"I have spent many an evening with Mr. Kidwell," I reply, knowing what she will hear in these words, and pause.

She stiffens beside me.

"He is a raconteur of the first order, especially after a few glasses of whiskey. The tales I have heard from his lips are more colorful than anything in the works of Mr. Dickens. He likes nothing better than an audience for his reminiscences, and he must have told me a hundred different tales, each one even livelier than the last."

"Kidwell?" Tildy says.

"Yes, Tildy, our very own Mr. Kidwell. In his youth he was a rustic guide in the Adirondack Mountains. He wore jerkins and a coon cap on his head, after the fashion of Daniel Boone. He fancied himself quite the man of nature, he said, and one afternoon decided to bag a moose for the delectation of the New York City guests staying at the lodge that employed him. Several of the guests, delighted at the prospect of a hunting expedition, asked to accompany him. Mr. Kidwell, who had as yet never even seen a moose, vainly consented."

Tildy lies quietly beside me.

"The little hunting party quickly became lost in the woods. Night fell, and Mr. Kidwell made up a story about moose being mainly nocturnal beasts. He promised his famished guests a dinner of moose roasted over an open fire—which, incidentally, he had no idea how to build. With the darkness came bitter cold, and the party huddled close for warmth under a bough beside a large boulder, where they fell asleep. Morning dawned, and they had just begun to stir when the boulder shook itself and stood up. The boulder was a moose, and it bounded off into the woods immediately, though it was in no danger from the hunting party. To a man they had run off screaming, terrified of the beast they had just spent the night with."

Though upon hearing Mr. Kidwell's tale I had been beside myself with laughter, Tildy does not even chuckle. Instead she sighs wearily and rolls over, putting her back to me.

"Tildy, most people would find such a story to be hilarious," I suggest.

I tell her about Mr. Haines, making light of our nighttime raids. I tell her about my stargazing visits with Madame Svetlana, the absurdity of us, two women, tripping around lost in cornfields in the middle of the night. I tell her of Mr. Pete's valiant failed efforts to teach me to stand on my head. Tildy responds to none of it.

I move close to her and slide an arm around her waist.

"Sugar lump," I say, and rock her a little.

No answer.

"My darling candy cane," I say, and rock her a little more.

No answer.

"Sweetie pie," I try, drawing it out a bit.

She only takes my hand, draws it up between her bosoms, and curls herself around it.

"Now that I have revealed all my secrets to you," I whisper, "are you not ashamed that you doubted me?"

IN THE MORNING, feeling refreshed, I take out my sewing box, a large, converted picnic basket, and open the lid. Inside its wicker walls, a riot of threads, yarns, and fabrics in shades of pink, green, purple, blue, red, and other colors bursts like a cornucopia of fruit. I run my fingers through the textures, silks and wools, jerseys and twills, for the sheer pleasure of the sensation. It gave my mother no end of vexation when I was a child, the way I preferred the company of our household servants at sewing time to the proper pursuits of a young lady of good breeding. Our Lady of the Looms, she would call me when she wished to discourage me. But I relished the name! After all, it was those coarse and vulgar girls, Irish or Negroes of little education, who could make things more beautiful than all the paintings that crowded the walls of our home.

"I think it is time I fitted you up for a new costume," I say as Tildy rolls over, rubbing sleep from her eyes.

"That so?" she says.

"Indeed it is," I reply. "Now you may have a suit of spotted leopard skin with fur trim around the collar. Or, if it suits your fancy, you may have the colors of a rainbow running all around you. Or—"

"Hold on, hold on," Tildy says, smiling and shaking her head at all the choices.

"Or," I say, leaning closer to her, "you may have a new fabric that I have only just spun during the night. It is so sheer that, in the proper light, it is transparent."

Tildy gapes at me. "Marie!" she says.

"But whatever your choice," I say, holding up a length of twine, "I must thoroughly measure you first so as to ensure a proper fit."

At this moment a clicking noise commences at the window. Tildy and I exchange puzzled glances, and then Tildy rises and goes to the window. She parts the dingy curtains and looks out over the backyard.

"What is it?" I ask.

She drops the curtain.

"Your husband throwing rocks," she says.

It is John, pitching pebbles at the window to get my attention. I open the window, and he shades his eyes as he looks up at me. He is dressed in the same type of suit he goes off to work in, the same leather shoes.

"Marie, I couldn't wait until evening," he says. "Please come down."

I close the window and shrug on a robe. Tildy won't look my way.

"I must put an end to this," I tell her. "I will return in a moment."

When I open the front door, he is waiting for me. I close the door behind me and take a step toward him. He is close, much closer than he came to me the evening before. I can smell his shaving soap, see the strands of his wavy brown hair.

"I couldn't wait to see you," he says again, and he bows his head as if his weakness shames him. Then he looks up at the house and his pale face wrinkles. "What are you doing here, in a place like this?" he asks.

I walk down the path to the road to put a distance between us and the boardinghouse. He follows me, and we stop at the road.

"John, you must listen to me. I cannot go with you."

He takes my arm and draws me closer, and I wish that I had not come out in my dressing gown. But it is too late now.

"Marie," he says, "we are man and wife. Haven't I given you everything a wife could ask for?"

I nod my head, as I must.

"Then come home, please."

I see, then, the motorcar he has arrived in, parked down the road not far from us. His lackey has accompanied him this morning and leans against the fender, watching us. The door sits ajar.

"No, John."

"Does this amuse you? Is that it?" He steps back from me and looks around at the barren road, the run-down house. "I'll buy you a cottage in the country, if that is what you want. You may even have it to yourself, if you like."

"Don't be silly!" I laugh. "You would never—"

But he is quite serious.

"Marie!"

Tildy has come out, fully dressed.

"Is that your maid?" John asks. "I'll hire a girl for you, solely for your wishes, if it will make you happy. Say you will return with me."

I stand there, suspended between them, for moments on end. My two poles, my former happiness and my present one, my John and my Tildy. The morning is still quiet, clear and bright, full of promise. It is almost like a dream.

Then the lackey stands and walks toward us.

"John, who is that man?" I ask.

"Nobody. A driver."

He continues toward us, and I become frightened. I look for Tildy, and she steps toward us as well.

"Please send him away."

"Stanley?" John laughs. "Why should I do that? Let me introduce you."

"No," I say, and step back from him.

"Marie, you all right?" Tildy calls.

"Yes, yes," I say, but in truth I am not, not with this Stanley approaching me in a way that disturbs me.

I run to Tildy. John stares in astonishment, then turns and halts his Stanley with a flick of the hand. A simple gesture, and another man stops as if he has been frozen into a photograph. That is the power at John's fingertips.

"Take me inside," I tell her, and we turn and scurry back into the sanctuary of the boardinghouse and shut the door behind us.

My heart is fluttering so fast that Tildy must help me into a chair. I cling to her arm, trying to regain my breath.

"Are they gone?" I ask when I can breathe again.

Tildy parts the curtains and tells me that they are.

"Well," I say. "Then it is over. Over and done." The palpitations have made me downright giddy. "My land, Tildy!" I can't help exclaiming. "That was quite an encounter!"

IN THE AFTERNOON, Tildy and I stay close to the backstage tent. Tildy believes it is safer to do so, and for the better part of an hour I manage not to stray too far from her. I tack a spray of fake flowers to a straw hat for Mr. Kidwell and replace some buttons for Mr. Pete. But in time I run out of things to do.

"Tildy," I say as we stroll for the hundredth time past the stage, "let us go and pay a visit to Miss Antoinette in her tent."

Tildy looks at me as if I have suggested roasting a child. "What for?" she asks.

"What does it matter?" I ask. "It is just a visit."

We stop and look out over the field. A blanket of dark clouds covers the sky, shading the sun. Out beyond the bench seats there is open field, and in that distant stretch of grass lies the tent of Sheba, Queen of the Nile. Past that lonely tent, there is another stretch of field and then row upon row of withering cornstalks stretching to the road and to the horizon.

"You don't need to go wandering over there," Tildy says, as if she is now my mother.

"Tildy, for heaven's sake, it is broad daylight!"

"It was broad daylight this morning, too."

"And I have come to see that I overreacted. It was my husband who came calling, not Jack the Ripper."

Tildy sighs. "When he come back again," she says, "you gonna tell him 'no' for real?"

Now I am offended. "What are you saying? I have told him 'no' already!"

"Like you mean it?"

She stands there waiting for an answer, as if she has asked me a perfectly reasonable question. But I am weary of the way she tries my patience, and I walk away without answering the obnoxious query at all. I pick up my sewing basket from a bench as I pass and march straight out into the field without a backward glance.

Once I reach the tent, I stop to catch my breath. The sounds of preparation are faint out here, carried to this place by a fickle and shifting breeze. The tent is quiet, and I realize that it is early yet and

Miss Antoinette may not have arrived so soon. I stand on tiptoe and try to see the black car that she usually rides in, but from this distance all of the cars look the same to me, and I give up.

The ticket stand in front is empty. The gay banners strung over the entrance sway lazily in the currents of the breeze. Had Tildy not chosen to be so insolent, I might have drawn her into a conversation with Miss Antoinette, though I must confess, in the few talks we have had I was forced by necessity to supply almost all of the commentary. But I am nothing if not patient, and she remains for me the central mystery of Doc Bell's Miracles and Mirth show, the most fascinating of all of the performers because she is the most inscrutable. I will not be satisfied, I will not rest, until I have engaged her and found out her heart!

I am reaching for the flap over the entrance when a hand from behind me clamps over my mouth. An arm, also from behind, grabs me around the middle, roughly pinning my arms to my sides, making me drop my basket.

I squirm to get free, but the arms hold me tight. A scream rises up my throat, but the hand suffocates it before I can get it out. Panic grips me. Who is this? Is it John's Stanley, sprung from a hiding place just as Tildy feared? Oh, Tildy! You were right! I twist and scream again, scream her name over and over, begging her to somehow hear my cries.

He drags me around the corner of the tent to where, I realize, nobody will be able to see us. Then the ground drops away beneath my feet. He has lifted me! I kick and thrash more violently, seeing now his intentions. In front of us lies the cornfield, all twisted brown stalks and obscuring gloom between them.

"John is waiting for us," he says in my ear. "Shut up."

And though the mention of my husband's name assures me that I won't be harmed, my heart sinks. The black motorcar, the door opening to swallow me. Dinner parties, the same set of rooms day in and day out. Afternoon tea every single day. Genteel ladies, the opera or polite chatter my greatest entertainment. I cannot bear it. It cannot happen!

I struggle like a bearcat and get one arm free. My feet touch the ground again, but he tightens his grasp and wrenches my head back painfully. He speaks into my ear again, but this time I do not hear the words because I see Miss Lily! She saunters around the side of the tent and freezes, looking directly at us.

Run for help! I try to scream with my eyes.

Instead, she puts her fingers in her mouth, emits an ear-splitting whistle, and then rushes right at us.

We all three go sprawling to the ground. For long seconds, we are a tangle of writhing arms and legs, and the man's fingers dig into my arm, refusing to let go. Then I get loose, and finally freed, I crawl away, sobbing in great gulps of sweet air. I look wildly around for John, preparing to run, but he is nowhere in sight. Miss Lily and Stanley twist and writhe in a ball on the ground, and I cannot tell who is getting the better of whom. But others are running across the field toward us now, Mr. Fleet, Mr. Rafer, Mr. Carmoody, even Mr. Pete, and Tildy.

The men fall on the struggling pair and Tildy runs to me. Once John's Stanley is securely pinned, Mr. Rafer and Mr. Fleet exchange a few words and come to where Tildy and I stand watching. Mr. Kidwell has hobbled across the field by now as well, followed by Madame Svetlana, and they all gather around me, these kind people, to make sure I am well. Yes, yes, I tell them, I am fine, I am unhurt. They reach out and pat my back to comfort me. They close around me so that they are all I can see, they and Tildy. They surround me, these people I have come to know better than my own relations, to tell me that I am safe, perfectly safe from harm, among them.

TOO SHAKEN to go onstage at showtime, I retreat to a corner of the backstage tent and listen to the others perform. Without me, Tildy abbreviates her performance to make up for the lack of the patter that I usually provide. We conclude earlier than usual and retire to the boardinghouses.

In our room, there is only a single chair and no couch. Tildy leads me to the bed and we sit, exhausted and fully clothed and shod. She puts her arms around me and rocks me and, though I haven't made a sound, says, "Shhhh, shhhhh, it's all right." And I hear my heart, thudding still in my chest as if it will burst its enclosure and break me into a million pieces. In time my Tildy's rocking and shushing works its magic, and my heart calms and comes to rest in its normal rhythm.

But I keep to myself the thoughts that continue to trouble me. John will persist. He will not settle for being thwarted. He will return, he will follow us, he will inject himself into our little society no matter where we go, he will disrupt the free and easy intercourse of our affairs. Even if neither he nor his lackey ever lays a finger on me again, the idyll of my season among the troupers and roustabouts of Doc Bell's Miracles and Mirth Medicine Show will never again be the perfection that it was to me.

In time the sound of snoring tells me Tildy has fallen asleep. Poor lamb, she has been through a great deal these last few days. I gently undo her arms, lay her down and stand over her, watching her sleep. As it was from the first, I cannot help but admire the firmness of her, her full lips, her solid brown skin, the curve of her bosom and hips, more voluptuous than she can ever imagine. For all my powders and frills and bows, the richness of her beauty is something I, a white woman, can never achieve. I can only hold it, and even then, finally, I must concede that some part of it eludes me, slips beyond my reach.

I unlace and pull off Tildy's shoes, then draw the threadbare coverlet over her. How terrible is the form we assume when we do as our natures compel us. I take a small grip from a corner and place in it a few garments and other odds and ends I will need. I snap it shut as quietly as I can, so as not to wake my Tildy. I kiss her gently goodbye. Then I take to the road, hoping that one future day our paths may cross once again under more auspicious circumstances, mine and my beloved Tildy's, mine and my dear John's.

Blush

Lily Meade

———

SUNDOWN, and once again Lily is stuck at the tent of "Sheba, Queen of the Nile" for the night while Doc Bell's show goes on without her. Since Gert took sick and the boy that replaced her ran off, it's been Lily's job to hawk tickets to all the rubes who push and shove to get in to see Sheba, Queen of the Nile.

Lily stands out in front, under the banners and pictures strung across the tent, smoking a cigarette. From here she can see the whole showgrounds. She's been with Doc Bell for more than fifteen years, since '03 or '04, when she got tired of her folks and took off from home. For all those years, she's helped haul the boards and crates for the stage, put her hand in staking and pitching the canvas, carted prop trunks and barrels of Doc Bell's tonics, salves, and soaps to the backstage tent. She pinches the tip of her cigarette, flicks it away, and rolls another. She should be roaming the grounds with the other roustabouts now, doing the work it takes to keep the show running at night, taking care of the occasional troublemaker with a few choice words or a little fist when necessary. Picking a few pockets if the crowd is big enough. They're all out there now, Rafer, Goose, Willie, doing that. And she, Lily, instead of being out there with them, is here tending to Doc Bell's freak, because of a busted wrist that won't heal up.

Her calloused hands long for the weight of a hammer, the burn of good rope. She keeps dropping the small nickels and dimes that the rubes give her for their tickets. She loses track of how many she's let into Sheba, Queen of the Nile's tent, though Felix Conger told her again and again: no more than ten at once, let the others wait, let them get all hot to rush in, better for business, blah blah blah. Well, that nitpicky little Jew bastard's not around anymore, and she doesn't care. She leans on the stand and hands out tickets and watches the herd of farmwives and mill workers and brats stream in until the tent won't hold any more of them.

A dim figure approaches and Lily stands up straight. When the figure gets close enough for the torches to light it, she sees it is Rafer, and she jumps down off the ticket stand at once. She must be getting sent back with the fellas finally. Rafe and the others can't be getting much done without her. Healthy, Lily can equal the work of any man, two on a good day.

Rafer stands there in that way of his that looks like leaning even when he's standing up straight. Hands in the pockets of his dungarees, head hunched forward, red hair lit up by the torchlight.

"Doc Bell wants you here permanent," he says.

Lily gapes at him in disbelief. "What? I ain't no goddamn barker!"

Rafe looks sympathetic and shrugs. "Doc says keep your mouth shut if you want. Just get Sheba here and back and sell tickets."

"And who's gonna pull my weight, huh?" Lily asks, disgusted. "Tell me that."

Rafe rubs at his temples. "We hired on a new man yesterday. Got it all covered, Lil."

There's a shout somewhere near the stage, and he goes off without waiting for her answer. Lily spits out the butt of her cigarette, steps on it, and fishes through the pockets of her trousers for the makings of another. But she's out of tobacco, flat out, and there's nothing for her to do but stand there fuming. She's got it in her mind to go find this new fella who's taken her spot and run him off straightaway. She and Goose and the others would laugh about it for years. Doc would have to let her back with the gang.

But there are people coming out of the tent, more clamoring to get in. Lily rubs the bad side of her face absently and climbs back on the stand, putting this new fella out of her mind for now. She'll find him when she needs to.

LATER, WHEN the show's winding down for the night, she puts out the torches and goes inside the tent to fetch the freak to the car. It's pitch black in the field when they emerge from the tent, and the freak stumbles across the uneven ground, holding on to Lily's arm. Lily would like to throw her in the grass. It's not that she's afraid of freaks, like some people. When she first got a look at this one, the gigantic head, full of water, they said, and the funny forehead, folded over like a lip, and those eyes that stared right through you, it didn't faze her at all. But this one's a nigger woman on top of it all, and Lily doesn't cotton to waiting hand and foot on a nigger, no matter what she does in the show.

Still, when they get to the car, she opens the door and settles the freak inside on the backseat. Then she goes around front to get the automobile going. It's an old Willys-Knight, a bastard of a car. In June the crank threw back on her and wrenched her right hand almost off her arm. The German wrapped it up and told her to rest it, but when is she supposed to rest? She grits her teeth against the pain, throws her weight in with both hands, and brings the car to sputtering life.

She's about to get in the driver's seat when she hears it. Tangled up in the ribbons of voices that drift along on the wind from the other vehicles, an unfamiliar voice. Nasal, thin, pesky. She slams the car door and walks on, toward it, sure it must be the new fella.

She passes a few cars full of rowdy performers waiting to be driven to their boardinghouse for the night. There's just enough light from the vehicles' lamps for her to see her way. At the next car, she finds a knot of fellas talking as they sling crates into the back of a motor truck. There's a kerosene lamp perched on the lowered gate of the truck, casting a glow over them all. Wiry old Rafer. Goose, bald and grinning as usual. Shy Willie, hanging back a bit. And the new one.

He's tall and hollow, a scarecrow in a flour sack. His hair stands on end like a knocked-over pile of hay. What he's saying doesn't bear being said. It's just a string of *uh-huh*s and *yeah*s and *you don't say*s to the other men's talk. For a moment, listening to it, Lily hesitates. Then she plunges forward.

When she gets close, he smiles at her. He has teeth like a horse, big and blocky. He sticks out his hand.

"You must be Miss Lily," he says. "I heard about you. Pleased to meet you, ma'am. Anything I can do for you, you just let me know."

Lily looks at the stuck-out hand, then around the ring of familiar faces, which look as baffled as she is. What does he think, that she's some kind of basket case or something?

"Name's Riley Jack, ma'am," the man says.

Goose, crouched on the gate, points at his forehead with an index finger. "Riley Jack was off fighting the Huns in France. In the Somme." He smirks again. "Ain't that right, doughboy?"

At this the man shuts up abruptly, takes back his hand, and goes back to his loading. He mutters something inaudible under his breath.

Goose giggles and disappears into the dark maw of the truck.

It's Rafer who pulls her away, down the road a bit. They stop after a few yards, the noise of distant commotions swirling around them in the dark.

"He ain't right upstairs," Rafer says, handing her a cigarette and lighting one of his own. "But he works for next to nothing. Said nobody else would take him on." He sucks the cigarette hard and long, as if to get something more than smoke out of it.

Lily could have guessed it. She's seen lots of men like him, fellas so shell-shocked they wouldn't know to open their pants before they piss anymore.

"That strawhead won't last a week, Lil," Rafe says. He grins in the moonlight, which is brighter now, and punches Lily in the shoulder. "You'll be back on the gang before we shove off. You healed up proper, now?"

"You old goat." Lily laughs. She spars with him for a moment, landing next to nothing, but enough to make it look like she's fine. Then Rafer takes her in a headlock and says enough, he's exhausted.

Lily backs away, pointing a finger at him. "I'll go easy on you, old man," she says.

Then she's cloaked in the dark again, wrapped in the noise of rumbling engines and tires rutting the road and the calls and shouts of the show wrapping for the night. Where she belongs.

Still, she can't help but chuckle at this Riley Jack, or what's left of him. Nobody's ever called her "ma'am" in her life. She walks along the shoulder, handling the word in her mouth, till she tires of it, ridiculous as it is, and spits it in the grass.

THE NEXT AFTERNOON, when she's sick of pasting labels on bottles of Doc Bell's meds and picking up trash and the other easy chores she's been relegated to by day, Lily drives out to the nigger boarding-house where she's supposed to fetch the freak and keeps going. The Willys-Knight growls underneath her, biting at the dirt road, eager for more, and she gives it a punch of gas. At this rate, by the time the freak gets up and comes out, it will be nearly dusk. Too many times Lily's sat around waiting for her, standing by the car, smoking one cigarette after another and watching half-dressed pickaninnies sporting around the scraggly vegetable patches that flank the boardinghouse steps. She's wasted enough of her time there. She'll swing by early evening, nearer to show time.

She drives on and parks along the road above the showgrounds, which are mostly quiet, and looks for him. Riley Jack. She shades her eyes with a sunburnt hand and scans the grounds, the tents, the stage, the vehicles. Rafer and the rest are down there, and a few performers, that bigmouthed Ma Fleet and her skinny husband, the medium Svetlana in her black dress. No sign of Doc Bell, as usual. She has half a mind to track him down and complain to him directly. Lily hitches up her trousers, pulls up a weed to stick in her teeth, and heads down the hill.

The fellas are standing around with shovels and pickaxes out behind the backstage tent. Riley Jack is there among them. He tips an imaginary hat to her as she approaches, and she ignores him.

Rafer nods at her, the rest say nothing. They've just started digging a trash pit, Lily sees, and she climbs in back of one of the trucks and finds herself a shovel without being asked to join in.

They dig for half an hour, time Lily loses herself in. The pain in her bad wrist becomes a hum, a blade, a seam of metal running through her. The muggy air leaves her covered in sweat, sweat that mixes with the film of dirt they raise in the air and turns her gritty. She forgets the freak, the tickets and coins, Jack Riley or Riley Jack or whatever he is. When she first hired on, Doc Bell laughed at the thought of her working for him. Back then, there was no Conger, nor half the acts Doc Bell has now. Doc Bell's Miracles and Mirth Medicine Show was a small affair, six or eight people all told plus a couple of horse-drawn wagons. Lily herself was right off the farm. Back there, behind her, lay her parents and their henhouses and pigs and chickens. Her mother fretted every day about the prospects of marrying her off. Sat many a night with her lady friends around the stove, knitting, yakking about how hard it was with a girl like Lily. How awful hard with a daughter that hated dresses, that never would fix up her hair or even look at a boy. And then there was that face, the left side of it frozen since a fever when she was three. A hard daughter. And the women nodded, nodded, whipping their thin fingers around the yarn and *tsk*ing sympathetically.

Well, see how hard it is to be shed of me, she thought when she walked off one afternoon while hanging laundry. Not hard at all. But it was harder for Lily to find someone to join up with. She hitched a few rides, got away, but found nobody who wanted her for work she was willing to do.

When she saw Doc Bell's Miracles and Mirth show crawling through a wheat field, she resolved to join it. Dilapidated wagons, swaybacked horses, a lousy bunch of hosers, her mother would have said, those show people watching stone-faced as the countryside went by them. *They* couldn't turn her down. But Doc Bell did. So she trudged along behind the weaving, jouncing wagons until night fell, and then she broke the bench seat on one of their wagons with a stolen axe.

They grabbed her, several men, and had her up against a tree. They might have done her in if Doc Bell hadn't appeared then, towering over them all, glowering down at her. Let me fix it, she pleaded. Let me fix it. And he did. She patched it with some saplings and whatever tools she could find in the back of the trucks. What she didn't know from working on farm fences and cribs and cisterns and coops, she made up as she went along. It held through the next day, and she was in.

Until now, anyway. Now this Riley Jack is among them, keeping her out, even though she has just proved her bad wrist won't stop her from doing her work. She's mulling this when Rafer calls for a break and sends Willie for a bucket of water, which they pass around, each dipping a drink as the bucket reaches him. As they sit talking and cooling off, Riley Jack gets up and comes around and sits next to Lily.

Doesn't he understand she has a beef with him? She looks at him, and he smiles at her.

"That hurt you any, ma'am?" he asks.

By reflex, she pulls the bad wrist close, hiding it. He must have been watching her, and she'd like to deck him for it. But when she looks up into the hollow face of Riley Jack with its dim trace of freckles under the tin-blue eyes, she doesn't.

He puts a hand against his own cheek, and she instantly understands. It's not her bum wrist he means. It's the dead half of her face. The other fellas have stopped talking and turned to watch to see what she'll say.

She gets up and walks off. Only when she's almost in the dry cornstalks rattling in the breeze thirty feet behind the stage does she get her wits back. She walks in without looking behind her, without turning to see Riley Jack's reaction. To hell with him.

A few rows in she starts to calm down. She turns around in a circle in the corn, muttering to herself. Then she heads back the way she came, but something stops her at the edge of the corn. Her face is tingling. The dead half. She puts a palm against it, puzzled. She hasn't felt anything there in years. Slapping it, pinching it, even touching a flame to it, did nothing. She stands there frowning, probing with her fingers.

Down by the ditch, the fellas are rising and picking up their shovels. Lily sees Goose behaving oddly and wonders why. He hasn't picked up a shovel. Instead, he's weaving in and out of the others, working his way over toward Riley Jack. Goose is always horsing, playing around too much. She has half a mind to yell something at him, like, *Leave that half-wit alone and get your keister back to work!* Riley Jack is standing there with his shovel, looking off in the wrong direction to see Goose approaching him.

Then Goose raises his hand and Lily sees the black, sinuous shape dangling from it and understands what's happening. It's what they always do to the new man, the little pranks the fellas play to test him out. Lily had forgotten. Goose comes up behind Riley Jack and grabs the neck of his shirt.

No! echoes through Lily's head, but it never leaves her mouth. Goose has already dropped the snake and Riley Jack has commenced to doing a jig. He clutches at his back, jumps around, and finally runs off howling and yelping into the corn a few yards from where Lily has emerged.

The fellas are all laughing, falling all over each other they're so tickled. Lily looks from them, to the corn, to them again, every muscle in her legs wanting to join them. But she plunges back into the corn.

A half-dozen rows in, and she can't hear anything, not the fellas laughing nor Riley Jack, either. There's no sign of him. There's no way she'll find him. He's probably bolted halfway to California by now. Still, she presses through the stalks, lets the dry, razor-edged leaves slap and cut at her as she pushes them aside.

She sees him, first, as a jumble on the ground, like a pile of rags. Then she gets through the last row of corn and kneels beside him. His shirt is torn. He is so still. Is this what happened when a man's mind exploded? Goose's foolishness has backfired, they've wrecked what was left of this Riley Jack for sure. That's not what she wanted, not how she wanted to get rid of him. One bony knife of a shoulder sticks up from the pool of wrinkled cloth, and Lily grasps it to roll him over. When she does, his eyes are wide open and unblinking.

"That wasn't nothing but a black snake," she says to him.

Finally, he blinks. "Yes, ma'am."

He watches her but doesn't get up.

What kind of man can't stomach a black snake, she thinks then. They aren't poisonous, don't even bite.

While she's thinking this, he reaches up and grasps her hands and pulls her down on top of him. Folds her arms around him like she's a blanket, tucks them under his bony ribs. By the time she realizes what he's doing, she's spread out over his chest and face, her cheek beside his temple. She freezes. Something spills out of her shocked mouth, but it isn't coherent enough to be words. She's about to yank herself away when she feels it: his trembling, shaking up through her, disturbing her down to her bowels.

LATER, LILY stands around outside the nigger boardinghouse, watching loafers come and go, watching the womenfolk toting laundry, smoking and waiting. Sometimes she swears she can feel herself going soft, and she presses her own belly or leg, wondering how quickly the lack of real work could make that happen. Then she dismisses the problem. In a few days, she'll get back in the swing, doing her job. Rafer is right.

As the days go by, though, she gets antsy. The locals ask her stupid questions, the freak comes dragging out later and later, nobody tells her to come back. Lily drives like a whip, getting them to the showgrounds in no time. Then the freak takes her sweet time getting across the field, even with Lily doing half of the walking for her.

Then the freak does something odd—pulls right out of her grip as they're crossing the field. Lily stumbles forward, turns around, and looks at her. The freak is standing there in her huge black hat, staring right back at Lily, the cane she has started using planted like another leg in the ground.

"Come on, keep up! I ain't got all day!" Lily snarls.

The freak just stares at her. She's already in her costume for the show, the crazy red frock that comes down almost to her ankles, black patent leather shoes, fake jewels. And the big black hat festooned with ribbons and bows like a float in an Armistice parade. It's ridiculous, all that finery and the huge, misshapen head the hat only partly hides.

"You coming or not?" Lily asks.

No answer. The freak has never said a word to her. Lily doesn't even know whether she can talk at all. Maybe she's an imbecile, though the way her eyes track Lily, watching every move, suggests otherwise.

"Fine," Lily says, tossing down her cigarette and stamping it out. "Suit yourself."

The freak can set herself up if she wants it that way. Lily doesn't care. She marches off to get coins for making change.

Once that's done and she's checked the tent's riggings, she has nothing to do but sit at the ticket stand, waiting for nightfall. Up on the road, the honking and braying and yelling of the locals starting to arrive is getting loud. It's nearly dusk now. Lily looks out over the field, where she last saw the freak. Best to make sure she's where she belongs. Lily gets up, flicks away the last embers of a cigarette, and steps inside the tent.

The gloom in there and the stuffy smell hit her at once. And that rasping sound of the freak breathing. Lily turns to go, stops at the doorway, and listens to it. It sounds worse today.

"You okay over there?" she asks.

No answer.

Lily wipes her hands down her trousers and walks over to where the freak sits in a kind of cubby made of canvas. No seeing her until you're right in front of her. Lily turns the corner and looks down.

The freak stares straight ahead as if Lily isn't even there. She's taken off the hat, and her head, like a huge rock sprouting grass here and there, seems to float above her body. Lily wonders whether all the rubes traipsing through all night ask the freak the same stupid questions they ask her before they go in. The satin dress shines in the weak light of the kerosene lamp at her feet.

"You want some water?" Lily asks her.

No answer. Just the rasping. Lily's wasting her time.

She turns and walks off. But when she's a few paces away, the freak speaks to her.

"No," she says.

Her voice is low and hoarse, lower than Lily's, but it carries clear across the tent.

Lily stops. Goes back. She stands in front of the freak again and watches as one of the freak's hands rises and straightens the high lace collar of the red frock.

"You want me to fetch you a bite?" Lily asks.

"I'm not hungry," says the freak.

Lily offers her a cigarette, but she turns that down, too, with the same lack of gratitude. Lily scratches herself. "Ain't that dress too hot?"

She waits for the freak to answer. But the freak just sits there, coughs a little, and then looks off across the tent like there's someone else there she'd rather be talking to. And that burns Lily, stokes her up hotter than she's been in a while, the implication that she's not even good enough to be tending to the needs of a nigger freak.

She throws her butt on the ground and stomps it. "That's it! I'm sick of being stuck out here in this goddamn freak show!"

She's halfway out of the tent when the freak speaks up clearly behind her.

"So am I."

Lily stops and turns around. She can't see anything in the dim light but the waving shadows cast by the lamp, huge and misshapen, on the canvas walls. "What—" she begins, but then she stops herself. What does she care what that's supposed to mean? Fuming, Lily turns and leaves in a huff.

Back outside at her ticket stand, she runs her fingers over the rough wood that gives her a few new splinters to pick loose every night. She shrugs, and laughs to herself, and decides to dismiss this uppity freak who must've let her lady-of-the-manor costume go to her head. What a laugh Rafe and Goose and the rest of the guys will get when she tells them about it. And as for herself, why, tomorrow she's going to go to Doc Bell and demand that he find somebody else to sell his goddamn tickets. Let that lazy boy Willie do it. He'd probably be happy to have an easy job like this, anyway.

She lights up a cigarette and makes no effort to keep the smoke from drifting through the tent flap.

A FEW EVENINGS later, she gets the freak in the car and steps around to crank the engine. The freak has become even slower, as if to spite Lily for talking to her the other day. Everyone else has already left for the boardinghouses.

When she gets in the car herself, she's sitting on something. She reaches down, feels roughness, stems, leaves. Lily turns around and glares at the freak. Is this some kind of a joke? But the freak pays her no mind.

It must have been somebody else who put it there. The fellas? She slides off the mess on the seat and picks it up to lift it out of the car into the moonlight, where she can see it better. What kind of joke is it they're playing on her, leaving weeds on the seat of the car like this? She turns the bunch of Queen Anne's lace and dandelions and buttercups and blackberries and grass over in her hands, puzzling over it, wondering what to do with it. Maybe they put bees in it. She looks closer, but sees nothing.

His hands come from behind her. The shock makes her drop the flowers on the road between her boots. His palms slide over the threadbare cotton twill of her trousers, spotted with oil, as if he is counting the threads.

"What the—" she begins.

She grabs his hands. He just stands there, behind her, breathing gently. Something in the stillness of him tells her he means her no harm, that she could let him go, and she does. But then his hands move again, over her hips. What the hell does he think he is doing, this crazy?

"How you like that bouquet, ma'am?" he says in her ear. "I know most people don't put no berries in their bouquets, but I thought you might like 'em."

She nods. She does like blackberries.

"Yes, ma'am," he says.

His hands move across her belly, toward her crotch.

"You just speak up if I'm making you uncomfortable now, Miss Lily," he says.

She nods again. Her voice seems to have deserted her. His hands undo her trousers, and the right one slides down inside her drawers. And for some reason, she allows it. His hand moves between her legs. Half of her turns into air. Her knees buckle. But he catches her, holds her up until her legs work again.

And then, just as quietly as he came, he slips off into the darkness.

When she trusts herself to walk again, she closes her trousers, wipes her eyes, gets her breath back, and gets in the car. The engine is still running.

Carefully, carefully, she pulls the big touring car onto the road. It is all she can do to keep it there, to keep it from running off one side or the other, as she drives the miles to the boardinghouse.

THE NEXT MORNING, Lily awakens to the sound of a rumbling engine and blaring horn. She rubs her eyes and sits up in the backseat of the Willys-Knight, where she spent the night. It's parked out in a side yard of the nigger boardinghouse, next to one of the vegetable patches.

On the road, one of Doc Bell's trucks is pulled over and Rafer waves to her from the driver's seat.

Lily gets out, shades her eyes against the already-bright sun.

134

"There you are! Been looking all over for you, Lil!" Rafer calls. "Come on! Get in!"

The canopy hides his riders except for the legs hanging over the back of the truck's dropped gate. She can't see who each set of trousers and dirty boots belongs to, but she is sure that it is the same gang she dug the ditch with. Goose, Willie. And Riley Jack.

"Go on!" she yells. "I ain't had nothing to eat yet! It's early!"

Rafer leans his rusty head out of the truck. "All hands on deck, Lil! We need everybody for this job!"

He's grinning, and he blows the ear-splitting horn again.

There's no way out. No way out of climbing in there, in the middle of them. She looks at her hands, but they look the same, creased and calloused as usual. Before she knows what she's doing she has put her hands on herself, checking that too. She jerks them away and marches forward, hoping nobody saw it even though she's not sure why it should matter.

It's worse in the truck bed. Goose and Willie are back there, along with Riley Jack, who is way in deep and shining a moony grin at her.

She settles in as far away from him as she can get.

For a while there is the usual conversation and horsing and bragging, though Lily finds she cannot let herself drift with it as she once did. Then, suddenly, Rafer pulls over at the side of the road, probably, Lily expects, to take a piss out in the corn. The chatter goes on uninterrupted until Rafer pokes his head around the back of the truck.

"Gentlemen," he says, "opportunity knocks. A chance for a bit of finery to perk up our wardrobes." He grins. "Look over yonder."

Everyone scrambles to the gate of the truck and looks out. Blue sky, white clouds, fields of withering cornstalks, and on the near slope of a grassy hill, a clothesline full of laundry out of the line of sight of the farmhouse it surely belongs to. Nothing more than a roofline is visible over the hill.

Goose and Willie scramble down from the truck without another word.

Lily manages to separate herself from the others and keep her distance. She takes a roundabout route through the cornfield, killing time, until finally she steps out into the open. There's not a stitch of clothing left on the line by then. The fellas have stripped it bare except for a lone sock that dangles in the breeze.

She heads back toward the truck. The dry leaves, slapping at her, feel less like cover than a curtain that might spring open at any moment, revealing the leering face of Goose, or Rafer. Something churns in the pit of her stomach. She realizes that showing up back at the truck last will only draw attention to her, curses, and breaks into a run.

But everyone's already there when she arrives, gathered at the back of the truck, showing off their booty. Goose is wearing some farmer's union suit over his clothes and dancing around in the middle of the road. Willie is sporting a pair of red suspenders. Rafer, watching it all, has several garments slung over his shoulder. He looks up as Lily approaches, and for the first time, Lily finds herself sorry that Felix Conger, and all his meddling and his rules against any hijinks off the showgrounds, is gone.

"You didn't get yourself nothing, Lil?" Rafer laughs.

She shrugs, but Rafer won't let it be. "Anybody got something to spare for Lil? Come on, you cheapskates. Look at all that. Willie, gimme that."

Lily sees Riley Jack standing off a bit, watching. Dressed in the same wilted, threadbare clothes he wears every day, he, too, is empty-handed. He looks at her, and she immediately turns her eyes away.

"Well, I got this," says Goose, and holds up a white cotton night frock with ruffles along the bottom. All the men laugh at him. "But I was gonna give it to Doughboy, here!"

136

He prances over and wraps it around Riley Jack's neck, and immediately Riley Jack blushes as purple as a wildflower.

"Naw, no," he says, trying to give it back.

"Put it on, Doughboy," Willie yells.

They start to converge on him, and a funny look enters Riley Jack's tin-blue eyes. He's still smiling, sputtering niceties, but his feet are backing away. Lily could tell the fellas to lay off, but they wouldn't. Kidding the new man is a ritual, and they'd wonder why she wanted to ruin everybody's good fun.

"You don't want my gift? Ain't you got no manners?" Goose jokes, and laughs uproariously at himself. Chuckles and guffaws echo him all around.

She hits him with a burlap sack full of tins of balm that was lying in the back of the truck. Goose dances back like a drunken marionette and tumbles into the roadside weeds. Lily drops the sack.

Willie runs over and pats Goose's cheek. He puts down his head and listens to Goose's breath. Then he sits up on his heels.

"That fool all right?" Rafer asks, breaking the shocked silence.

"Think so," Willie says as he gets up.

"Come on, help me get him in back and let's go."

For a moment they just stand there, though, both of them staring at Lily as if she just dropped down out of a cloud. Then Rafer and Willie gather up Goose's limp form and haul him to the truck.

Lily is the last to climb into the back of the truck. Nobody says anything, but they don't have to. Rafer fires the truck up and it lurches onto the road, and there's only the engine sound and the tires eating the road. Lily watches the coil of white frock sprawled in the road as it shrinks and shrinks, until it is too tiny for her to see.

THAT EVENING all of the rubes, every last one of them, make her skin crawl. Dragging scrawny children, shuffling along and whispering in their amazed voices, they come to the tent in paltry but steady numbers. There is never a moment without them, never a time when there are not two or three arriving to press damp coins into Lily's palm or shuffling out to stand around like cows in a field. Lily is exhausted by an hour past dusk.

Earlier, she managed to get away from the fellas once the truck arrived at the showgrounds and has not been near a one of them since, not even Rafer. But that cannot last. She won't be able to spend all her time hiding out with the freak or dilly-dallying with minor chores. She will get called on to work. It's what she asked for. So she resolves that she simply won't take any guff off of any of them. If anybody plays around, if anybody sasses her, if anybody pulls anything funny on her, she'll fight. After she's decided that, her mind rests a little easier.

Then one of the shadows comes out of the darkness and it isn't a rube, it's Riley Jack. He gets politely in line and when his turn comes up, he says, "I'm going tomorrow, ma'am. Soon's I get my pay, I'm shoving off. Why don't you come on along with me, Miss Lily? It'd make me happy, having you along."

"What are you talking about?" she says.

"I'm asking you to come with me," he says. "I'm leaving."

Then, like a box opening up, she understands him.

"I can't just go off like that," she says.

She beckons to the people behind him, and they come forward and pay and pass him by. He stands there, hair askew, hands in his pockets, watching her.

"Why sure you can," he says. "You're a grown woman. You can go where you want."

She thinks about it a minute, and it is almost enough to make her laugh. What does he think, that she is going to start wearing frocks? That she is going to learn to cook, and sew, and that she is going to stay in some house of his all day, tending babies?

"I ain't asking for nothing," Riley Jack says, "but for you to come with me. You think about that."

Maybe it would be easier that way, to just leave, to get away from the freak and the job of tending her, to get away from the fellas and the way they are bound to treat her different from now on. She can't go back to the way it used to be, she's sure, not after today. They won't let her be just one of the fellas again, not after she went and put herself out for Riley Jack the way she did.

"Hey, gal, you deaf? I said gimme three of them tickets!"

An angry little old man looks up at her, waving a fist.

She looks around, letting him stand there awhile. Riley Jack is gone. She looks down on the balding head, the horny fists, and tears off a ticket.

THREE DAYS later, she senses a commotion off a ways, out along the road. Lily has a hammer in hand, nails in her mouth; the ticket box, past mending, has gone to firewood and she is building a new one to stand on.

She has kept away from all of the fellas the whole time, but now that will end. It could be trouble. Boozers and rounders sometimes picked fights with show people just for the fun of it, or a firebug might try to put a match to a tent or one of the trucks, or maybe the local sheriff and his men might decide to bust a few heads to send a signal not to cross them. Lily gets up, puts the hammer down, and lopes off in the direction of the commotion.

By the time she gets there, Riley Jack is lying on the ground underneath the branches of a dead tree, the fellas ringed around him. One leg is bent up behind him like he was dancing when he fell. His head is turned to one side. His eyes are open. An arm is slipped beneath his own dead body.

"Dammit to hell," says Rafer.

"What that half-wit go climbing way up there for anyway?" says Goose, smiling. "We told him to come on down from there."

Lily looks at Rafer, but he won't meet her eye, and eventually he simply walks away.

"Must've slipped," says Willie, shaking his head.

Lily can see what happened. Up in the high branches of the tree someone has wedged a beat-up grip. Maybe they greased the branches, too. It is Tuesday afternoon, long past payday. He'd have been gone long ago, Riley Jack, that paltry grip under his gangly arm, if he hadn't been hanging around waiting for her.

She steps around them, straightens Riley Jack's arms and legs out, and drags him a ways down the road, away from the rest of them, and it is hard going. When she stops, there is a little trickle of blood coming out of his mouth, dribbling down one side of his chin, and she stares at it for a long time but does not wipe it away. She looks at his face, finally calm now. With her fingertips, she closes his eyes.

"Goose!" she yells. "Go get a blanket!"

Grudgingly, he trots off.

She will dig a hole and bury Riley Jack herself.

AS THEY ARE packing up the next morning to move on—to Robbin, Pennsylvania, Lily has overheard somebody say—Rafer comes over to where she is taking down Sheba, Queen of the Nile's tent.

"You're back with the gang, Lil," he says, smiling. "Doc Bell says okay, Willie can do this from now on. Didn't I tell you? When we get to Robbin, you're back on setup."

Lily looks up from where she's kneeling. "No," she says, "I'll stay here."

Rafer laughs at first, because he thinks she's ribbing him. Then, when she doesn't join in, he frowns at her. "Why, Lil? This Sheba thing ain't fit work for a pig."

But she feels no obligation to explain herself. She doesn't bother to tell him she's not doing it out of laziness or to spare her bum arm. It's where she belongs, now.

After Rafer goes off and leaves her alone, she bundles up the poles and canvas without help and carries several loads to the truck, where she stows them. All around, Doc Bell's Miracles and Mirth Medicine Show is collapsing. Tents coming down, the stage coming apart. Pretty soon there will be only a field of trampled grass and a few ditches and trash pits to mark their passing. And the unmarked grave, which she put at least a mile away from the rest, under a tulip tree.

She makes her way through bustling bodies to the Willys-Knight. She can see the black hat through the back window. They will have to wait for Madame Svetlana, who always takes her sweet time. Then all of them will ride in the car together, driven by Lily.

She opens the door and looks inside, finds that familiar gaze directed back at her from under the ruffled, beribboned brim of the hat.

In the driver's seat, she feels those eyes come to rest on her neck. Does her passenger know what has happened between Lily and Riley Jack and the rest of them? Why Lily is with her for good, now?

Lily's face is tingling, even the dead side. When she touches her cheeks, the heat of her own skin makes her take her fingers away. She knows what is happening, but she feels no urge to hide herself. If Doc Bell's people got a look at her now, what would they say? Would they whisper and point, like so many of them do about Sheba, Queen of the Nile? Like she used to do, herself? She no longer cares, not about them, not about the blush that has spread across her face, from her hairline to her chin.

The Circle

Ed "Pa" Fleet

———

ON HIS WAY across the field, Ed Fleet seems to pass half the members of Doc Bell's show as they ready themselves for the night's performances. He helps Kidwell with a heavy carpet bag, good for a wink if not a smile. "Feel like bootleg, Kiddy," Fleet teases, and Kidwell agrees. "Pennsylvania's best," he says. "South of Mason and Dixon, good batch of it might pass for piss." After Kidwell, it's Carmoody and Pete, then Madame Svetlana, roustabouts, a few others, and everyone stops for a word or a nod with Fleet. When he reaches the open-air stage, the colorful angel and mermaid flanking it, the sea of empty bench seats stretching out before it, Fannie beckons to him. She gathers up her holstered pistols and her flouncy skirts and squats at the edge of the stage. Sparkly earrings dangle from her ears, and fake diamonds glitter at her throat. She brushes back her blond hair and grabs his wrist. "I feel hot to you?" she asks, and places his hand on her forehead. "I don't want none of these ruffians touching me. I think

I got a fever." Fleet smiles. "Don't know about a fever, gal," Fleet says, "but ain't nobody hotter."

They've been having up nights and they've been having down nights. This one looks to be an up night. Clear sky, folks in good enough moods, and for that Fleet is thankful. Good days have been few, and he sees the toll. He sees the tiredness in hands and feet, hears the hope gone from laughter, the out-and-out fear in the little snipes and jabs Doc Bell's people trade more and more these days. They will pull through the last few weeks of this season, just like they've come through troubled times in the past. But it's been rough, rough on them all, and he'll be glad when they are headed south, bound for winter in Florida and the rest they all need.

He has strolled back out to the show vehicles to fetch his prop trunk when the black car carrying Lily and Antoinette pulls up and stops on the dirt shoulder. The two women get out, Lily scowling, Antoinette taking her time. Fleet walks down to them, interrupts them to offer his arm to Antoinette.

"C'mon, gal," he says. "Give a old man a hand."

She takes his arm, and they walk into the field. He doesn't jabber at her, the way he's seen people do and then get uppity when she doesn't fall in with their chatter. As if she's carefree as a child. He waits until they are halfway to her tent before he says a word.

"Fine night," he says. "Feel like fall in the air."

For a moment, there's only the sound of her labored breathing beside him.

Then she says, "Yes, it does." It is the way she converses with him—enough to be polite, but no more.

How many falls has she seen? He doesn't even know her age, really, where she is from, or even how she got to Doc Bell's show. So many things. Another four steps, and he speaks to her again.

"I hear we ain't too far from Deep Springs. S'posed to be mineral baths there."

She seems to consider this, but as is often the case with her, she says nothing, and he is left to wonder what she is thinking. Her grip on his arm tightens just a bit.

Fleet does not know what to say to her next. So they walk along without words between them.

At her sideshow tent, Fleet holds the flap open for her to step inside.

In the tent's damp interior, he watches her settle herself in her chair beside a lamp on the floor. She smoothes the folds of her frock till it lies flat on her lap, just like a young girl waiting for a suitor. He has not told her what his wife, Louise, tried to do to her and Haines and the others in the car with them that night. Recently he has walked her here from the car often, has checked on her during the evening and brought her water when she needed, has stopped by her room in whatever boardinghouse Doc Bell has put up his colored performers. It doesn't make amends, he knows. All he means to do is hold her hand, pull her just a little toward the circle of folks in the show.

Folks did the same for him many a time. And, he's shamed to say, they did it from the start, from when he joined up with shows, not weeks or months after. Back in '75, with his first med show, a little out-fit of only four or five folks, it was Simmie Baxter who did contortions and coochie dancing and who knew what else. She sidled up to him, all red hair and green eyes and red bow of a mouth, that first day. Laid a hand dead center of his fifteen-year-old chest and said, "Dumpling, you follow me." No white woman had ever touched him like that. And though his instincts told him a white gal like that was trouble, he fol-lowed. By the end of the day he knew everything he needed to know, right down to which tonics to pilfer when he wanted a shot of pure whiskey. Simmie could comb her hair with her feet, could reach over her shoulders and pinch her nipples with her own toes. She was fond of crevices and hollows, and liked to surprise you with the ways she could get into them.

There had been lots of shows before Doc Bell's. Hobart's Fresh Minstrels, Lubjohn's Dixie Peaches, Swell's Shines and Shimmies, Max Cukor, Parker's Picks. Some he stayed with for so little time he'd forgotten their names. But never the folks in them. He remembers every one of them. Like Jake Gilley. Little fella with a lazy eye. Jake could hypnotize anyone and anything—men, women, babies, chickens, goats. He'd get folks up onstage, talk them into a trance, and take their purses while the audience howled with laughter. If he could put out a chicken, he said, he got to keep it; and chicken was what he had for dinner many a night. From Jake Gilley, Fleet learned how to clear things out of his mind for a while so he could sleep at night.

Now, Fleet settles himself on one knee and puts a hand on Antoinette's knee. Under her black hat, her head is enormous. Poor gal, she's still got many of Doc Bell's people thinking she's simple because of it—that, and the fact that she hardly says a word to them. And, he's shamed to say, he thought the same for the longest. He knows better now.

"My wife, Louise," he says.

She watches him, silent.

He has to look down at her feet to say the rest. "That night. Night your car broke down and Haines, ah, went off and never come back." He lets his voice trail off, finds it again. "Was my wife that messed with the engine and made it cut out like that."

He glances up and finds she is still watching him, her dark eyes unmoving under her wide forehead.

"Louise was trying to get all of y'all lost. Get you left behind by the show. For good."

Now it's his breathing he hears, labored as hers, as he looks at her patent leather shoes. He's wheezing with the effort to get it out, finally, out in the open. He looks up at Antoinette.

"That's your wife," she says.

He waits, but she adds nothing to it. Does she mean that's your wife, that's Louise, all right, that's what she's like? It seems far too familiar, coming from her, so he doubts it. Then he believes he knows her mind. That's his wife, he understands her to mean—not him. Two different people. And he's thankful enough to give her knee a gentle squeeze through the slippery satin fabric of her costume. She's lifted a burden from him. Lifted one burden, and placed another on his shoulders without meaning to, a heavier one that makes him want to sink down on the floor right then and there.

But he doesn't do that. Instead he stands up.

"Anything you need?" he asks her.

She closes her eyes, and for a few moments she seems very far away. In her mind, is she off somewhere else, far from Doc Bell's show, from this squalid tent? He will have to show her sometime, sometime when they know one another a little better, what Jake Gilley taught him.

She opens her eyes. "No."

"I'm a try to swing by later," Fleet says.

Back outside, he stops to get a good breath. The field is a whirl of activity. The evening's show will start in half an hour. The stage torches are lit now, and the bench seats are filling with families: old folks, fidgeting children, babies in tow.

Suddenly he sees the field empty. Doc Bell's Miracles and Mirth Medicine Show gone, like it was never there. And his wife, Louise, standing across the field from him, her chin up, her hands in fists.

Then the vision is gone.

Lily comes around the side of the tent, toeing stakes and yanking the lines to test them. Her hair is a tangle, as usual, and a cigarette hangs from the corner of her mouth. How Doc Bell has gotten her to sit still and sell tickets to "Sheba, Queen of the Nile" all night, Fleet can't guess.

"You want a light, gal?" he asks her.

She squints at him like he's crazy, takes the unlit cigarette out of her mouth, and gapes at it.

"Well, damn," she says. "Sure."

He strikes a match from his pocket and she sucks unevenly on the cigarette.

"Sales don't pick up soon," he observes, "we gonna be eating those for dinner."

He can usually get a few words or at least a lopsided grin out of her, but this time she only grunts and marches off to finish her inspection. Fleet decides that will have to do. Folks are about as ready as he can get them, he judges. He's had a word with just about everyone who'll give a few moments of their time to an old man making his evening rounds.

SINCE FELIX CONGER took off some weeks back, Fleet's been in charge of the stage. There was a tussle or two over who would get what slot on the bill, and a few complaints from people who didn't like taking orders from Fleet, but Doc Bell backed him up and now folks do as he says. He knows all their bits, can read an audience. Tonight he has Fannie and her trick shooting at the top of the lineup.

There was a little fuss, too, when he took himself off the bill. Since then Louise has been doing numbers by herself and has stopped asking him when they were going to get back to their regular routines as "Ma and Pa Fleet." For twenty years they'd been doing their act together. Truth was, he didn't know when he'd be ready to go back to it. That was what he said when Doc Bell called him in for a chat in the back of the motor truck where Doc made his office some of the time.

There were clothes strewn around among the crates of bottles and tins, faint flowery scents mixed in with the sharp smells of tonics and salves. Obviously Doc Bell had had a woman or two inside not too long ago. Fleet settled himself on a crate.

"Rheumatism?" Doc asked. "That what it is?"

Fleet flexed his fingers, and they worked fine. "No," he said.

Doc Bell trained his huge black eyes more closely on Fleet. He was already wearing the black-and-white Quaker outfit he'd go out onstage in later, during one of the breaks in the show when he hawked his medicines. "The pay troubles? We likely be back to regular pay soon."

"No," Fleet said. "That comes and goes."

"People acting up?"

"Not no more, no sir."

Doc Bell sat back and frowned. "It's that Haines boy eating at you, ain't it?"

"Reckon so."

For a week after it happened Fleet and Felix Conger had roamed all over the countryside trying to find a trace of him. Before shows, after shows, north, south, east, and west, farms, crossroads, towns, mills, feed depots, every drain, ditch, and cellar they could find anybody in, they asked. Have you seen a Negro boy we lost, about twenty, round-faced and good-natured, honey-brown, little over average height, guitar on his back? Then one corrected the other on this last detail since Haines left his guitar in the car when he went tramping off in the dark to look for help. It was hard to imagine him without it, or it without him. Impossible to believe he would just abandon it if he had a choice.

They filed reports with constables and sheriffs, but none of them did a damned thing. It was like Haines went up like smoke. Except Fleet knew the kinds of goings-on that were happening, nothing new but bloodier this summer of 1919 than they had been for a long time. Just when it was simmering down in one place, it boiled up again somewhere else. In Washington, D.C., they dragged people off trolley cars and set fire to houses with children in them. Jails torn open, colored men chased down like dogs, mobs tearing people to bits.

Doc Bell sat up, absently fingered his broad white cravat, and gazed at Fleet gravely. "We been together a long time, Fleet. You know me. You know I stick with my people."

Fleet nodded.

"You know what-all I done for that boy. Everything I could. *Everything*. Never did take to his job, and maybe just as well he's gone..." Doc Bell began, then trailed off into his own thoughts. "But I got a flock of people under my wing here, and I gotta tend to them all. Keep the show going."

Fleet thought about this, then nodded.

"You know Strohmeyer's quitting after this season? Ain't but a few Kickapoo shows on the road no more, neither." Doc Bell frowned and shook his big head. "Ain't seen nothing like it since that farm depression back in the '80s. But we rode it out. And we gonna ride out the picture shows, and the Pure Food nonsense, and all the rest."

He leaned forward, offering his huge hand. Fleet took it.

"You take all the time you need. You always got employment with Doc Bell, least till they lay me in my grave."

Tonight, Fleet moves Tildy and her sword-swallowing act up to the second slot. Putting two novelty acts in a row's not normally a good way to go, but tonight the crowd needs the pep.

Over in the corner of the backstage tent, Kidwell is fingering a money belt. Doc Bell's doled out all kinds of chores since Felix Conger left, and though Fleet's kept his tongue about it, not much is getting done right anymore. Kidwell, for instance, is collecting ticket sales from the two sideshow tents a few times a night. Fleet thinks he's been skimming. Letting a boozer like Kidwell handle cash is like giving seed corn to a crow and hoping you'll get your fields sown.

Fleet sits down beside him, startles him though Kidwell isn't even doing anything yet.

"I knew a gal back in Kentucky," Fleet says, "had herself a beau she liked to keep out of sight. Kept him way in the back of her broom closet."

Kidwell stuffs the money belt under his shirt and tucks the shirt sloppily into his pants. Fleet's never seen him neat a day in his life, sober or drunk, and he guesses there's no reason he'd start to be now.

"Had her a second fella, too, as you might of guessed. Kept him tucked out of sight in the cabinet under the kitchen sink."

Kidwell's watching, now, out of runny eyes.

"She even got a third fella squeezed under the couch. And a fourth up the chimney, where he get black as soot. Number five's in the cold cellar and six's up a pear tree out in the yard. Seven's in the garden, where she got tomatoes growing thick as flies on a donkey's ass in summer. Needless to say, she don't weed that garden much."

Fannie pops into the backstage tent, and Carmoody and Pete step out on the stage.

"Eight's in the barn and nine's in the well sitting on a bucket."

Fleet stands up and stretches out his legs.

"Well, all right," Kidwell says wearily. "She's gotta have ten, right? Where's she stashed the tenth one?"

"Ten? Oh, he up on the roof. Give out a whistle whenever he see her husband coming down the road so the other nine can scramble back to their hiding places. You should see the ruckus with all them fellas tripping all over each other whenever ten sound off."

Kidwell smiles, then his grin turns sheepish and he fingers the bulge under his clothes. "Ain't no real secret what's going on, that it?" he asks. "Everybody knows what's up?"

"Yep," Fleet says. "They surely do."

Fleet goes out behind the tent and looks up at the sky, which is just now going fully dark. A few more days is all he asks. A few more days like this, no trouble he can't handle.

THE NEXT NIGHT'S even finer, clear and mild, more like early summer than the cusp of autumn, but it doesn't matter. Without Felix Conger around for folks to scrap with, they start grating on each other. Fleet can feel it in the air when he makes his rounds at dusk. He lingers a little longer, gentles his joking a bit, tugs at a few sleeves. Nevertheless, just as he's finished getting Tildy set for her first time on, he hears a commotion over by Antoinette's tent.

He slides off the stage and jogs over there. When he's close, he sees it's a couple of roustabouts clenched together, that bald hooligan Goose and the older one, Rafe, who ought to know better. Lily, hard to believe, is standing off to the side, watching.

"Hold up! Hold up!" Fleet yells, waving his arms. "Y'all step back! Let go, now!"

They ignore him. So do the few of Doc Bell's people who've gathered to watch. How the hell did a runt like Felix Conger keep a lid on things? Fleet wonders.

When he sees the first bloody lip, Fleet decides. There's no getting around it. He jumps in and tries to wrestle Goose away from Rafe. But the three of them are as tangled as a ball of string, and he can tell quickly that this won't get him anywhere.

"Gimme a hand!" he yells to anyone who'll listen.

Nobody budges.

Then somebody lands a punch and they all go sprawling. Goose falls on Fleet, knocking the wind out of him and gouging him in the gut as he scrambles to get back to his feet. Gasping, Fleet follows him. Where the hell is Doc Bell? He could part everyone with a wave of an arm, if not a simple command. But as is his wont, he's out of sight when he's not onstage.

"Svetlana! Go get Doc Bell!" Fleet yells.

Svetlana, at least, responds. She flies off in a whirl of black fabric.

There's blood on Fleet's shirt now. He can feel blows vibrating through Goose, rattling the man's bones. He senses that this is no ordinary scrap, that this time Goose won't back down till he's dead, and he has to get these people apart. Now.

He ducks and gets between them. For a moment, they all wrestle for position. Then a blow crashes into Fleet's cheek, and he goes down.

The ground comes up and catches him hard. Somebody falls on top of him. Then, finally, it stops and hands grab him by the shoulders, hands cup his head, voices call out his name. *Fleet! Fleet! You all right? Look what you done, you idiot! It wasn't me, it was you! Wake up, Fleet!*

He lies there, lets himself be handled, leaves his eyes closed. He doesn't want to look into their faces. Can't. He lets the yelling go on around him.

Then he feels he should open his eyes, and when he does, the circle of scared faces he sees calms him. "Get back and give the man some air," Lily barks, and though he does not really want them to, they draw away. "You okay, Fleet? Fleet, you okay?" Lily asks.

Antoinette is there, at the edge of the circle of faces, looking down from under the brim of her wide black hat. She must have heard people screaming his name, he realizes, and come out of her tent. Then his sight blurs red, he is lifted off the ground, and she vanishes from view.

They carry him to the backstage tent. By then, he doesn't need to be carried, though, and insists on walking in on his own two feet. They sit him down among all the chairs and tables draped with costumes and the brimming prop trunks. Hands behind him keep him upright. Kidwell gets down on one knee and, delicately as a nurse, swabs blood off Fleet's cheek with a grimy rag. "Can you see?" he asks. Fleet nods that he can.

At that moment Louise bursts in from somewhere and sees him bloody. She barges forward, looks around, elbows Kidwell aside, and for a moment Fleet expects her to snatch the cloth from him and try to tend to her husband herself. But her hand hesitates, and she draws it back before he has to say with more than his eyes, *Don't touch me.*

"What happened?" she asks.

"Nothing," Fleet says. "Little scrap. It's over now."

"Who hit you?"

Fleet looks at her. His wife's frock shimmers when she plants her hands on her hips. People step back and give her room. Though her face is skinnier now, though there is less to her arms and hips and legs these last weeks, her eyes flash fury.

"No matter," he says, and he gets up.

He waves people off, tells them to get back to the show. There's work to do. He's fine, yes, he's fine. He ducks out the back of the tent and Louise follows him.

"Go on, gal," he says over his shoulder.

She catches up with him. "Old man, you got to be more careful. You can't afford to be having accidents like that with these fools."

Since he's not going to shake her, he stops. There's worry all over her face, the worry of not knowing his mind as she has for years. But there's no ease he can give her about that.

"Louise," he says, and he makes no effort to soften the words. "It wasn't no accident."

And this time, when he walks away, she doesn't follow.

HE IS NOT Louise, and Louise is not him. Antoinette is right on that count, and Fleet can't avoid it anymore. Never, never would he have done the thing his wife has done, and it has separated them like nothing else could.

She didn't know what she was doing, he's told himself. *She didn't know it would lead to what happened*, he's told himself. *She never would've done it.* Not a thing like that.

But it's done.

And doesn't she know better? Show people had to be careful, no matter how nice the locals seemed to be. Stranding your own people out on a dark road like that, it was something you didn't do. Even in good times, no telling what it could lead to. Once, when he was a boy traveling with a little circus, some of the local hooligans caught up with Alphonso the Fire Walker and nearly burnt him at the stake trying to figure out the trick of his act. Man couldn't go near an open flame again after that, had to leave the business.

And what about Antoinette? What was his wife thinking, treating a sick gal like that just because Louise got the willies every time she looked at that sideshow tent? Ever since, he'd had one eye on the tent half the time, looking for Louise to go sneaking in there with some kind of mayhem on her mind. He couldn't believe he'd see anything like that, and at the same time, he thought he might. If he hadn't been gray before, watching that tent would've been enough to make him so.

This morning, he's got a few minutes to kill, and he walks down the threadbare hall of the ramshackle boardinghouse where Doc Bell's colored performers are staying. There's a slight rotten odor coming from the kitchen at the other end of the hall, where the mistress of the place, a fat yellow gal name of Martha, is busy trying to fry something for the afternoon meal. Fleet's glad he'll miss it.

He knocks on Antoinette's door, waits a decent pause, and then opens it slowly.

She's standing in the center of the room, dressed in a worn, gray cotton frock, the black hat with all its ribbonry perched above her eyes.

Puzzled, he walks to her, asking if everything is okay.

"Yes," she says, and moves toward the door. He takes her arm, asks if it's a breath of air she wants. "Yes," she says, and they leave the dim, close, dirty room together.

As they pass through the rickety front door and into the yard, where a few heads of Queen Anne's lace wave among the knee-high weeds, Fleet can feel her breathing right through his arm. A ripping sound that seems it could cut off your hand. He wonders what it feels like inside her.

But he doesn't ask, merely lets her steer where she wishes to go, which turns out to be out along the dirt road, opposite the way to the showgrounds. On either side of them lie fields full of corn and wheat stubble.

He is fishing for something to say when she asks, "Does it pain you?"

It does not escape him that this time, she has started a conversation. But he doesn't know what she means. Though it makes no sense, he thinks of *her* breathing, *her* swollen, heavy head, *her* limp. Then he realizes she must mean *his* eye, which is bruised and still weepy from the fist she saw him take.

"Just a touch," he says, and he smiles to show her there's no lasting damage. "Pains me worse to see such a thing happen."

They walk in silence for a few moments more, then he finds himself telling her a few of the goings-on that are on his mind. The way the jobs that Doc Bell handed out to people after Felix Conger left are all mixed up, the problems that's causing. Just yesterday they opened what should have been a shipment of salves and found spinning tops inside. She comments on none of it, but he believes she listens to it all.

"Folks doing their best," he finishes just as they arrive back at the boardinghouse.

At the side of the road, a car sits idling, waiting for passengers. Rafe sits at the wheel, too sheepish to look Fleet in the eye a day after the scuffle. So Fleet goes around to the driver's side window, flicks up the brim of his hat, and says, "No point trying to run me over while I got one good eye left to see you coming." That gets a smile out of Rafe. "I'll tell folks you're out here waiting," Fleet says.

Then he takes Antoinette back inside to her room. At the door, he says he'll see her later. He's already turned to go when she says, "Thank you." She closes the door before he can say there's no need for that.

When he climbs in behind Rafe a few minutes later, he sits beside Louise, as usual. She has stopped asking him where's his banjo. He no longer carries it.

"How you sleep?" he asks, though he shared a bed with her and knows perfectly well she tossed during the night.

"Good enough," she says.

"Look like a clear day," he says.

She sighs like a sudden breeze on a dead calm afternoon. "If all you got to say to me is that bird-chatter nonsense," she says, "you might as well not say nothing at all."

They ride the rest of the way in silence.

IT'S A GOOD crowd gathering for the night's show, Fleet sees as dusk is falling. And yet, he doesn't have a good feeling about this evening.

Three acts into the show, Fleet hears the audience rustling and slips around behind the backstage tent to see why. Uniformed officers are fanning out through the crowd near the stage. Fleet stands perfectly still until he's found and counted four of them. Probably some of those state constables he's heard about. About the right number for busting up the show, smashing every crate they've got of Doc Bell's tonics and potions with the excuse of a "search" for stolen goods, and cracking some heads before hauling half the troupers to the county lock-up on some trumped-up charges till Doc Bell pays to spring them all. This hasn't happened in years, not with Felix Conger seeing that the local authorities were paid off every place the show landed. Fleet has no idea who Doc has doled that job out to, but whoever it is clearly hasn't handled it too well.

Fleet sticks his head back in the tent and beckons Pete outside. He sends the little acrobat to fetch Doc Bell, wherever Doc Bell is. "Find him fast as you can," Fleet says.

Before he can turn around, Fannie is behind him, clawing his arm. He spins and sees her powdered, white face glowing in the darkness.

"You gotta knock me down a few spots," she hisses. Six-shooters jostle in her hip holsters.

"What?" Fleet asks. "Why?"

"I can't go on next!" she nearly shouts, and he can see she's losing her wits, is too rattled to hit the stage. So he goes in and switches her with Louise, who doesn't protest.

Pete comes back while Fleet's in the hushed backstage tent, peering through the stage flap to see what the officers are doing.

"Can't find him," Pete says.

Fleet sends him off to look again. How hard can it be to find a seven-and-a-half-foot-tall white man in the dark? He doesn't want anyone bigger and easier to spot than Pete running around the grounds, but maybe Pete's not bright enough to track Doc Bell down.

The constables, though, have settled in. They sit among the audience members watching the show, and you might think they were out for an evening of fun if it weren't for their folded arms and the way they throw glances among themselves every time a new act comes on. Still it puzzles Fleet, why they're waiting so long to bust things up.

"What's holding them?" Kidwell, beside him, asks.

"Don't know," Fleet mutters.

Fannie jumps up from a corner, then, and rushes at the two of them. "Fleet, put me on after Doc!" she demands.

"What for?" Fleet asks. "It's another two acts before Doc Bell go on, and one of them is you, gal. That's the way he want it. Now what you want me to go against his orders for?"

Her eyes are big, frightened, scared of more than just what it looks like is coming.

"Fleet, please," she begs.

But Pete's still gone and without him, his partner Carmoody is stuck backstage. Fleet's got no choice but to send her on, so he does.

As soon as she steps out, the officers perk up. They look back and forth at each other, passing some communication between them. Fannie stumbles out and skips around the front of the stage, twirling her pistols around her index fingers to get the crowd whooping and hollering. Then she sets up to shoot over her shoulder with a shaving mirror at a row of bottles on the far side of the stage. For a moment she's okay, chin up in the air, working the crowd with her smile. But the constables, one by one, start to rise to their feet.

"There's Doc Bell," Kidwell says, and Fleet peeks out and sees him striding over from the sideshow tents in a white suit that seems to glow in the dark.

Pete pops in through the back flap, and everybody in the backstage tent crowds behind Fleet and holds their breath, waiting to see how Doc Bell will save them from the trouble that's brewing.

The officers rush the stage, and Fannie bolts. Heads turn, people start to rise off the bench seats. A buzz of muttering turns into shouting and full-out commotion as people rush from the bench seats pell-mell, knocking them over as if they are fleeing from a fire. In the midst of it all, Fleet can see Doc Bell wading in, his long arms outstretched, his mouth moving as he tries to quiet the crowd. But nobody pays any attention to him.

Fannie dashes into the backstage tent and out the back flap, a whirl of powdered ringlets and white skirts. A constable bursts from the stage into the tent, wielding a pistol, and looks around wildly. Somebody screams. He bowls right through them and out the back, touching nobody on the way.

Louise's standing at the back wall, still as a carved Indian. "Stay out of it, old man," she says.

Fleet runs outside.

Around him, it seems all hell is breaking loose, but not in the way he expected. The crowd is swarming over the backstage area now, converging on the show vehicles. They reach them and climb up onto them, trying to see by moonlight the chase going on farther downfield. There, Fannie is running for a field of withering corn, hair and skirts flying, two faintly visible officers close on her heels. It's a toss-up whether they will catch her before she makes it. Screams and shouts spiral up into the night air. Over at the vehicles, one of the motor trucks is rocking as a gang of young men tries to tip it over. Doc Bell is nowhere in sight, and even if he were, Fleet knows, not even he could stop this now.

The crowd swirls around Fleet, jostling him, making him throw up his arms and struggle to keep from being trampled. Then a thought strikes him, and he pushes through the crowd to where he can see the sideshow tents. Neither Svetlana's nor Antoinette's is still standing.

It takes him forever to fight his way through the roiling bodies and reach the first tent. The field around it has emptied, and it lies crumpled like a fallen bird. Fleet drops to his knees and lifts the canvas, crawls under into the airless space beneath, calls Antoinette's name. There's no answer.

He wrestles the tent over, leaving its exposed poles and riggings sticking crazily in the air. There's nothing underneath. Antoinette is gone.

A screech of metal and wood draws his eyes to the stage and the tent behind it as they collapse into a heap. He sees nobody come out of it. He can see nobody from the show anywhere, not even Doc Bell. Out here in the field, under a beautiful, crisp night sky, he is alone.

ALONE. He remembers. That summer he and his little brother Elson set out from Connor, Kentucky, because with both of their parents gone for over a year now, there was nothing to keep them there. By themselves they took to the road. Many colored folks were doing the same those early years after freedom, walking during the light hours and sleeping beneath bushes and trees at night, living off mulberries and blackberries, the occasional squirrel and biscuits from strangers who took pity on them and had a little to spare. There was nothing unusual about two boys, thirteen and nine, tramping along with their worldly goods tied in cloths slung over their shoulders.

Only they had no destination. Fleet didn't even know, at first, what direction he was leading them in. Elson, wiping his nose on his sleeve all the time, would fall behind. Fleet would find he was talking to himself, stop, turn around, and wait for Elson to catch up. In fits and starts like that, they moved down country roads, across meadows filled with wildflowers, through woods swarming with gnats and into little towns of no more than a few houses and a store or a church.

To slow himself down further, Elson played harmonica when he walked sometimes. Between songs he liked to imitate things with it, train whistles, bird calls, the buzz of a saw in a mill. Sometimes he drifted into a ditch or tripped over a rock, he was so preoccupied with the harmonica. Fleet himself knew how to play nothing and thought Elson's harmonica a waste of time.

"Keep up," he'd say. "You fall in a pond, I ain't fishing you out."

"I ain't ask you to," Elson would reply, unperturbed.

After a while he started asking Fleet where they were going. Fleet had no idea, but he didn't say that.

"Mama got some people out in Virginia, I think," he said.

"That where we going?"

"Quit asking me that."

"It ain't no crime to ask."

"From now on, it is."

Fleet fashioned a hundred fishing lines from bits of thread and scraps of metal, nails and pins and fence wire that they found on the roadside. Sometimes they spent whole afternoons trying them out.

"You ain't gonna catch nothing with that," Elson would laugh.

"Watch me," Fleet would say.

Usually, nothing was exactly what he caught. But on one occasion he got a shiny black catfish fat as a piglet from a stream that didn't look deep enough to cover anything that big. They got it up on the bank and watched it thrash around until it died, both of them too afraid of it to go near it.

"That thing so big we ought to give it a name," Elson said.

Instead, they ate it, every last white, sweet bit of its flesh, after they roasted it over a fire. Neither was hungry for a whole day after that. They lay in a field of clover, saying what they saw in the clouds that floated over them.

They might have gone on forever that way if Fleet hadn't felt a chill in the air. It was September, and summer was running out. Elson didn't need to ask where they were going for him to know he needed to answer that question.

When they ran across a set of tracks stretching off decisively into the distance, it seemed like the best thing to do was get on a train. Fleet knew people hoboed out on freights all the time. You had to look out, not get caught, because the train people didn't like it. They might throw you off or beat you up if they found you. He'd have to be careful, especially with Elson, who didn't have a lot of sense when it came to practical things.

He watched for several days until he knew the way the trains came through. They slowed to a crawl just as they reached a bend in the tracks that fed onto a bridge over a small creek. There was plenty of brush growing on one side of the tracks, good to hide in. On the other side was a wall of rock, wet and mossy because no sun fell on it.

"I don't want to," Elson said.

"It be easy. I'm a show you how," Fleet said.

They waited for a train, and Fleet explained how it should be done. He would go first, run and get up some speed, and hop on an open car. Then he'd get Elson's arm and haul him up. Elson wouldn't have to do anything but run.

They lay in the brush while a train went by. Elson didn't say anything.

"Next time's for real," Fleet said.

When they heard the rumble, they gathered their shoulder sacks and hid in the brush. Elson had the harmonica in his hands.

"Put that away," Fleet told him.

The train appeared from around the bend and Fleet took off. Was this one going a little faster? Or was he imagining it? It was harder than he expected to catch up with the open car he'd spotted. The ballast alongside the tracks was poor ground for running, and the ties were even worse. When he finally got to where he could grab the car and haul himself in, he was thoroughly winded.

Elson was still running.

"Come on!" Fleet called.

Elson caught up, raised a hand, and immediately fell back.

"No, you gotta keep running!" Fleet yelled.

He turned around and looked to see if anyone on the train had heard him, but the noise of the train had drowned out his voice. Had Elson heard him?

Elson caught up again, and this time Fleet grabbed his hand.

Immediately, Elson stopped running.

Stopped in space as the train continued moving, Elson dangled in the air, his feet gone out from under him. His weight nearly pulled Fleet right out of the car. The blow knocked the wind out of him. The train shifted and started to curve around instead of away from the two of them. Elson dangled like a rag doll for a moment, and then he drifted under the train.

Fleet felt his brother yanked from his hand, and Elson was gone.

He leaned over the edge of the car. Nothing. He leaned out, tried to see farther back, to find Elson lying beside the tracks. Nothing there, either.

Then the train was clattering over a bridge that crossed a stream, and Fleet had to wait, crouched at the open freight car door, until it lumbered onto the opposite bank.

As soon as it did, he jumped off. He ran into the cold creek, waded through the deep middle, and scrambled up the rocky bank. The many cars of the freight train were still rattling past, and the tremendous racket and the motion made it hard to find the place where Elson should be. Fleet ran back and forth, beating the brush, but there was nothing.

So he stood there, gasping for breath, waiting, waiting, until all twenty-some-odd cars of the freight train had passed him by. His eyes and ears fastened on every useless thing in range, the flash of leaves in the sun, bird calls, the Southern Pacific and Union Central names painted on the sides of the cars. Finally the last car rumbled past him, and there was silence.

Elson lay on the tracks, bloody, mangled, still.

Fleet didn't believe it. Just a few minutes ago, Elson had been complaining, they'd been running after a train. Things could not be so different that fast.

Later, when he went back out to the road and sat down at the side of it, he still could not believe it.

The next morning, when a caravan of circus wagons came out of the distance and rolled one by one past him, he did not know what to think. He was about to get up and go back to the tracks and look for Elson.

The last wagon stopped, and a Negro man with quiet eyes and a cat's grace swung down.

"You lost, son?" he asked Fleet.

Fleet just looked at him. The man turned and said something to a woman peering out the back of the wagon.

It was the Willis-Listo Circus. The Negro man was Small Long-street. He played banjo, mandolin, accordion, fiddle, and piano, and inside of a year he would teach Fleet how to play them as well. He could whistle a tune through one nostril, and he taught Fleet how to do that, too. He could walk on his hands, he could carry his wife on a chair balanced on his feet as he walked on his hands, and he could balance their daughter on his wife's shoulders at the same time. He taught Fleet to do these things with such patience that Fleet, in time, learned them all, and much more.

Never, since then, has he been without a show.

Now, amidst the ruins of Doc Bell's Miracles and Mirth Medicine Show, he moves like a wind-up toy along with the few others who've stayed on the showgrounds, assessing the damage, seeing what can be salvaged. Fannie—Alice Mott, as it comes out she called herself, or Dora Gue, or Enid Murphy, depending on her mood—is in jail for stealing the money purses of respectable gentlemen after plying them with her favors and drinks laced with knockout drops. Married men at first, who had cause for keeping their mouths shut when they found out. Lately, though, she'd gotten sloppy, and it was whoever she could lure, any gentleman with money.

Antoinette is safe, spirited from her tent by Lily. Svetlana the medium turned up a mile away, cowering in a melon patch. Nobody's hurt, not by anything more than bumps and bruises. Fleet finds an ice pick, recognizes it as the one from Matilda's prop trunk, and drops it in the sack over his shoulder.

"Ain't but a minuscule setback," Doc Bell told them after it was all over. "Important thing is, wasn't no fire. Fire eat up a show like nothing else. But we got most everything we need. Just a matter of putting it all back together, and I know ain't none of you gonna back down from a little hard work."

In the back of a motor truck, they ride under the canopy in silence as the new day dawns unbearably bright around them. The ride feels so long that Fleet briefly forgets where it is they are supposed to be going. It is like they are going nowhere. The blank, shocked faces of the men and one woman he sits with echo the same thought to him. When the truck stops, and he stands facing the boardinghouse where Louise lies sleeping, it is minutes before he goes in.

She lies on her back, one hand thrown over the side of the bed, snoring softly. He comes close, stands over her, but she doesn't stir. She doesn't know he is there. It is a very, very long time that they have been together, and yet he has never stopped to observe her like this, sleeping like a child.

"Aw, Lou," he says, and turns away.

On top of a chest of drawers, his banjo lies. He lifts it down. Funny that it turned out to be lucky he did not have it with him last night. He touches the strings, and they feel not like strings but like wood under his fingers.

He steps back out in the hall, the banjo hanging by its neck at his side.

At Antoinette's door, he taps, waits, and goes inside.

It is dim, the shade drawn. She sits in a chair beside the bed, a loose turban wrapped around her head. Fleet walks over and sits on the bed, but she doesn't look up at him.

"Hell of a way to get a day off, ain't it, gal?" he says.

She doesn't speak.

"What is it, gal?" Fleet asks.

He waits for her to answer, and the wait stretches out far longer than usual. She lifts a fist and presses it against her mouth.

Whatever it is that is worrying her, it is a worry he can't begin to imagine, what is in it, what it feels like for one so afflicted. After all the time he has spent with her these past weeks, he could not even guess.

166

All of his strolls and chitchat, what use could all that be to someone in her place?

He sighs and lifts the banjo and plucks a few notes. Not a song, just notes. They flit through the gloom of the room and sink into the walls. He strums a few more, and when those are gone, he begins to play a song, "On the Morrow," slow so that it will last longer than usual. When that is over, he plays another. When he looks at her she has closed her eyes, and her hands rest on the arms of her chair. He wonders whether he ought to stop, whether he is only tiring her. He knows so many songs, hundreds of songs.

He is just beginning "Quinces and Pears" when one of her hands lifts from the arm of the chair and her fingers open, as if she is guiding a flow of ribbons or thread through them. He slows his tempo again. He is accustomed to people nodding their heads, tapping their toes, grasping hands and reeling across the floor, but this hand is something new to him and he finds he is nervous, like a first-timer, like a boy marking each string separately, as he did before he understood he was playing one instrument.

Her eyebrows slacken. Even across the bulge of her brow, he sees it clearly. Should he drop the banjo and make sure she is all right? He doesn't know whether she will collapse, will tumble right out of the chair onto the floor in front of him and do herself even greater injury than nature has already inflicted on her. But her hand remains open, her fingers thread the music, and he shifts, instead, into "The Ballad of My Remorse" and slows it, like he has done the others, until it is little more than air.

When Fleet is done with this song he stops. Antoinette's eyes stay closed, her hand remains as it was. He stands and walks his old bones to the door, opens it gently, and slips quietly out.

Back out in the hall, there is still no activity though it is early morning. Not even a smell of cooking food. But folks will rise soon. They will go to the showgrounds and repair the show and more than likely be ready by tonight. They will get along without Felix Conger, without Fannie, for a while, anyway. And as long as they do, he will make his evening rounds.

THAT NIGHT, they put on a show. There are pieces missing, for sure, but it's a show. Fleet and Louise ride back to the boardinghouse, and when they arrive, Fleet takes a walk by himself.

When he returns, very late, she is sitting on the lone front step.

"Gal, what you doing out here?" he asks.

"Can't sleep," she says, and scoots over so he can pass through the door.

His wife. She is his wife. He reaches down, takes her hand, leads her inside to their room. He closes the door behind them.

He lights a lamp, turns it down low. She stands where he left her.

He comes behind her and unbuttons the back of her sequined frock slowly. Her breath comes in jerks and starts, but she says nothing. When he's made the garment drop in a puddle at her feet, he reaches around and takes her breasts in his hands, cupping them gently. Then he lets go.

He lays her on her back in the bed, strips her undergarments away. Last, her shoes. She seems to be barely breathing. But she shudders faintly, once.

Then he stands over her, looking at her body, avoiding her eyes. He opens his pants and sighs. It is necessary for him to reach in, handle himself. Then, fully dressed, he straddles her.

At the first stroke, a moan escapes her. And at the second. Her breath grows jagged, and she grasps his wrist where it is planted on the bed. He shakes her hand loose, takes her wrist, pins it to the bed beside her head.

Harder, faster. The backs of her thighs are a wall he bores through. She is gasping, noises tumble from her, she is saying something like his name, but not his name. Then her back arches, her knees lock around him and she bucks against him.

When she releases the grip of her legs, he continues, tracing his eyes over her collarbone, the line between her breasts, the sagging mounds on either side. Harder, faster. He wonders whether she will cry out, push him off. But she does not.

Then he spends himself, slows his body. He lies down beside her.

After a few moments he shifts, and she jumps like something has startled her. He rolls over and faces her, looks deep into her eyes. Gathers his wife in his arms, enfolds her as if he will never let her go. He burrows his face into her neck and kisses her. Kisses her so hard he believes the mark will stay there for the rest of her days.

Medicine Days

Antoinette Riddick

———

ALMOST DUSK. Smoke scents the air, and Antoinette lifts her nose to it where she stands just outside her tent. It would not surprise her these days to find Doc Bell's medicine show swept by flames. Since the riot, there have been nights when it only ran for an hour. They no longer stay anywhere for more than three or four days before they move on, often in the middle of the night to avoid paying the bill for their lodging. And they bicker and scrap with each other constantly. Since she keeps to herself, she overhears it off in the night or through the walls of her room.

Tonight, there is no fire on the grounds that she can see, and that is a relief. Once she would have been untroubled by the sight of fingers of flame tearing down the stage, the tents, every last scrap and shred of Doc Bell's Miracles and Mirth Medicine Show. That was back at the start, when she thought herself to be a visitor among the members of the show. When she believed that she would return to the Dunham

Hospital for Incurable Children, where she had lived the whole of her life before Bell.

She had misunderstand her position when she first found herself dressed in red satin, shod in patent leather, housed in a bannered chamber and visited by strangers who stared open-mouthed at her. Well, hadn't she always been stared at? Hadn't she always drawn attention? At Dunham Hospital, hadn't doctors taken her every measurement, written pages and pages of notes, stood within her hearing and spoken in amazed voices? *How old, now? Remarkable!* Nurses had stared, clucked, stood with their hands on their hips. *And you can walk, can you? And talk? And figure, too? Well, now, isn't that a miracle!* Even the visiting parents looked long and hard at her as if making silent comparisons, as if thinking, *This child can walk, this child can talk, while my poor lamb lies moaning, wailing, burning with fever!*

So she thought she knew why she had been directed to sit in a tent, why crowds of people came to gaze and sigh and point their fingers at her. Until the night that she told the show manager, Felix Conger, that she was tired and wished to return to the Dunham Hospital for Incurable Children, and he laughed at her.

"Listen, gal," he'd said, "if it wasn't for Doc Bell, know where you'd be right now? The Wooten Asylum for the Colored Insane, that's where. They're the only ones who would've taken you. So don't act like you're the Queen of England with me."

A hunched little shadow, barely bigger than a child himself, he struck a match against the crate he was sitting on and lit a cigar. "Bet you don't know what they do to cases like you in a place like the Wooten Asylum, do you?" he asked, puffing acrid smoke. "Bet you got no idea. Well, let me tell you."

And he did. Things so horrible she did not believe him. By the time he got up and ground out the butt of his cigar with his heel, she had stopped listening to him. "You wore out your welcome at Dunham Hospital, is the problem. What are you now, twenty? Twenty-one?

Long time since you were one of those sad little moon-faced babies, ain't it?"

As the days and nights dragged on without change, the truth of her situation sank in. She could not return to the place she had come from. This was her life now. What she'd taken for a visit had in fact been her delivery into Doc Bell's show. A nurse at Dunham Hospital had dressed her in woolen stockings and shoes and a coat one night and taken her in the hospital's ambulance to a place alongside a dark road where a car was parked. "You go with these men, now, and do what they say," the nurse had said, and patted Antoinette's shoulder. She had not been afraid. Strange doctors had come to Dunham and examined her, talked to her, even taken pictures of her, many times before. One looked her over cursorily now. After he was done, she had pulled the rough coat tight around herself while wind whipped through the few trees nearby and shot over what she thought was an open meadow beyond them. The ambulance, a rattling old hulk with a white cross painted on each side, sputtered off into the darkness. She had not even known to wave goodbye.

She walks around to the front of her tent and sees the source of the smoke: a distant bonfire, probably someone burning trash. Doc Bell's Miracles and Mirth Medicine Show, her only home now, will last for at least one more night.

ONCE SHE understood that she was to remain a part of the medicine show—a name that made no sense to her, that had no relation to all the singing and dancing and clowning that Doc Bell's people did at night—her days became slow and clear and sharp as a knife.

The raw spring cold seeped into the tent at night and grabbed at her arms and legs. The blare of music outside entered her ears like sticks. The mornings became an endless procession of foods she could barely eat, cracked plates of it set on the floor just inside the door of her boardinghouse room: a bit of egg and bologna, or a pool of watery grits, often cold. And those rooms themselves, filthy beyond anything she had ever seen. She recoiled from touching the soiled bedclothes, the streaked and gritty windows, even the grimy floor.

And the show people. Spending her waking hours in rented rooms or the tent, she rarely came into contact with any of them. But she observed them. They talked loudly, never stood still, and dressed in clothes that looked to have been plucked at random from piles of dirty laundry. The one named Lily drove her daily to the showgrounds but barely spoke a word to her. The rest eyed her warily or turned away when they met her in the hall of a boardinghouse, as if she carried a catching disease. If one treated her kindly on occasion, he soon stopped, as she expected Mr. Fleet to do eventually. The snatches of lectures she'd heard from her tent convinced her, in time, that even Doc Bell was just another of the clowning stage acts, like the pretend policemen or sailors in the troupes who sometimes visited Dunham Hospital to entertain the children. With that knowledge, she resigned herself to her new life among these strange people.

If she did not grow used to her new companions, she at least came to know what to expect, which made the days a little easier.

SAUER WAS another thing she came to expect. Every few weeks he arrived with his bag. At first she was confused as to whether he was a real doctor or was just pretending, as the rest of them did. But she quickly saw that he knew how to auscultate her chest for lung and heart sounds, to check the dilation of her pupils, to test her patellar reflexes, to do just as the doctors at Dunham Hospital had done to her all of her life.

In place of days, months, seasons, Sauer became the ritual that marked her time. She let herself be carried by the rhythms of his tests and measurements beyond the walls of her room to clean, polished floors and white-tiled corridors broken by tilted transoms and hung with signs she knew by heart. DISPENSARY. CRITICAL WARD. KEEP

174

QUIET. EXAMINATION ROOMS. The smells of alcohol and camphor and sterile gauze, the sounds of clinking instruments and rattling bottles and squeaking metal carts, the dry taste of furnace heat rising from floor grates as the Dunham Hospital boiler fought back against the first blast of winter. HYDRO-THERAPY. She had watched the polio-stricken carried here, or wheeled in, wrapped in their blankets from head to toe. And the paralytics, and some whose maladies she could not discern, who cried and moaned whenever they moved their bodies. J. HOWELL HARVEY IRON WORKS, ELMIRA, NEW YORK on the metal plate in a corner of the laundry room, where the heat from boiling vats grew so intense she could scorch her fingers just by knocking on the door. And MILLS BAKING FLOUR stenciled in black on the barrels that sat in a row outside the kitchen, where the cooks, if they were busy enough, would let her watch them stir their huge pots and listen to their talk of husbands and children. She closed her eyes and counted the sparrows that gathered for shelter on the deep sill of the window beside her bed. When Sauer came to her, she returned to Dunham Hospital for Incurable Children in the only way she could.

But as the summer heat rose, she felt a change coming over her. At first, she saw bright lights in the darkness and heard the rush of wind on calm days. Then her cough worsened until her breath became an animal lodged in her chest. Her legs at times threatened to give out under her. The pain in her head never ceased. She thought of the children she had watched at Dunham Hospital who thrashed and wailed in their beds, then moaned and whimpered now and then, and finally lay barely stirring behind gauzy nets that nurses entered with trays of food they only carried off later, untouched. And then, one morning, the empty bed. She watched Sauer listen to her sputtering breath, grunt to himself, and throw his stethoscope back in his bag. Waited for him to order her to swallow pills or some bitter spoonful, as the Dunham nurses did, or to grab her arm and plunge the slow burn of a needle into it, as the Dunham doctors did. But Sauer did none of these. He continued his visits as if nothing had changed.

After the bitter disappointment of the orange-haired Negro doctor, she had drifted through gray reveries for days before she came back to her senses. She had waited for the one thing she could rely on, Sauer's visits. But as the days, then the weeks, dragged on, it became clear that even Sauer had abandoned her. He did not return, and her days became boundless.

EARLY ONE evening at the showgrounds, just after Antoinette has pulled herself out of the backseat of the motorcar, she sees the head of a man rise like a sudden moon over the canopy of a nearby truck. He steps into full view, and she stares at the size of him, like nothing she has ever seen. He is a man and a third high, with black hair spiked on end and a hand scratching it that could serve as a plate. His outfit of loose white trousers and shirt with a double column of brass buttons down the front nearly blinds her as he comes near in the twilight and walks right past where she stands on the line between road and field.

Then the man turns around and Antoinette senses that this must be him—Doc Bell—the one whose unseen hand moved the show from this town to that and set his people to dancing and singing or made them stop. The one who gave them their dirty boardinghouse rooms. The one who sent Felix Conger to bring her among them. He takes several long steps down into the grass and looks out across the field at his show coalescing in the gathering darkness.

"Ain't she beautiful?" he says over his shoulder. Then he turns and looks at her.

Before Antoinette can answer, he walks back toward her. The field is a bowl of grass that begins at the lip of the road, and when he pauses again a few feet away, he stands just low enough in it that she can look up at him without breaking her neck. But his height still dizzies her.

176

"You getting enough to eat, gal? You sleeping warm and dry at night?"

He is talking to her. His face is shadowed by the fading light of the sun somewhere behind him, but she can see his eyes on her, alert, waiting.

She has been getting enough to eat. She has been warm and dry at night. So "Yes," she finally manages to say.

"Good. Now, these cowboys and Indians of mine been treating you good? They been behaving themselves like I told 'em to?"

He winks at her and grins. Then he looks past her at Lily, who has yet to come from around the driver's side of the car, and says, "I expect not. But don't mind 'em too much, gal. They ain't never been to finishing school and learned their proper table manners and elocution and what-all. And some of 'em's a little simple. Ain't that right, Lil? But Doc Bell ain't never been too high and mighty to mix with every kind that God put on this green earth, from the lords and ladies right down to the rubes and pickaninnies, and anybody you ask gonna tell you the same. Doc Bell sticks with them that sticks with him. You can count on it."

It all sounds, to Antoinette, like the rapid, jumbled, nonsense mutterings of someone burning up in a fever dream. All of it but the last. *Doc Bell sticks with them that sticks with him.* And what other choice does she have, now that he's made her one of his people? She has never thought of herself that way until now. She takes a step backward from this towering man, which presses her against the side of the still-warm car's fender.

Behind Doc Bell the stage torches flicker and the seats fanning out from the stage shimmer with the shapes of arriving men and women and children settling in one after another. He bows his head slightly, as if he is thinking. "You know, people ask me, they say, 'Doc Bell, why don't you just quit? You been at it near as long as Sunday been a day of rest, and with the Pure Fooders after you, and the picture houses sucking up all the rubes, and a Vocalion warbling in every parlor, there ain't no place for med shows like yours no more.' They tell me, every thing got a season, and yours is just about up. You know what I say?"

He's looking past the stage now, at the stubble of a harvested cornfield beyond it. It's almost offhand, the way he speaks, as if he is just chatting with himself, as if he is not paying attention to who might be listening to him. And yet, as soon as he stops speaking, the air around Antoinette seems restless with his question. She swallows. Does he expect an answer?

He goes on without one. "I tell 'em, I may be weary in my bones, but I know, I *know*, a butterfly can go back to being a fresh young grub once again. Who's to say it can't? Who among us can claim to know all? *Who* is to say that just because Ponce and Leon ain't found it yet there can't be some fountain of vital juices flowing right down to this day, and that some of us don't know how to tap it? Great War ain't shut down Doc Bell's Miracles and Mirth and neither did the Spanish Plague. And I'm here to tell you, gal, *nothing ever will*."

He ends quietly, so quietly Antoinette must strain to hear him. *Nothing ever will.* It registers with her, finally, what she is seeing: the level, steady manner of a few of the older nurses at Dunham Hospital—never one of the doctors, always a nurse—the ones whom she would notice calmly handing to a doctor the tweezer, or the bandage, or the chloroformed gauze he wanted an instant before he asked for it. The wind flows around Doc Bell, fluttering his sleeves, flapping his long pants legs like flags. He turns back toward Antoinette and drops his hands into his pockets in an easy way. "Course, some folks, they say Doc Bell ain't nothing but a confidence man, that he's just another fraud. You think that's true, gal? You think I ain't no more to be trusted than a rat among the fresh-laid eggs?"

This time when he pauses, like the dropping off of a steady wind into a sudden calm, she knows he is waiting for an answer. And she is accustomed to answering: doctors, nurses, cooks, and chambermaids, all of whom addressed her with their straightforward, businesslike questions. *Did you take your castor oil today? Where did that Jenny girl get to now?* But this question of Doc Bell's is not nearly so simple to answer truthfully or to meet with a lie, either one, because she does not know the answer, does not know what this man is, whether simple truth and lies as she has known them even exist here, so filled is she suddenly with all the confusion of her last months. His question nudges her forward, opens her mouth, raises a pulse in her ears that grows louder the longer she is silent.

He ends it with a hand that he claps on her shoulder so heavily it nearly pulls her over. His voice falls down from above her, through the mesh of her hat brim, a hiss, a sigh, a whisper.

"*Course* I ain't to be trusted, gal. You can say it out loud. *Course* Doc Bell ain't to be trusted."

She can't say it. Not out loud. But to herself, in her mind, she approaches his words, hesitates, touches them.

And as if he has heard, and is satisfied, he lets her go. She watches as he steps back once, twice, three steps into the field, and the white of his suit shimmers like a moth flitting past a lamp.

"Truth is, ain't hardly no honest souls in this entire world," he says, "because ain't a *one* of us is pure. Not Santa Claus, not President Wilson, not Jesus Christ hisself. Hell, you think that loaves and fishes act wasn't the original sleight of hand? *Course* it was. The only *honest* man, gal, the only *pure* man there is on this whole topsy-turvy planet, is the one that'll admit flat-out to you that *he ain't to be trusted.*"

Doc Bell raises one arm and points. "Look out there, gal, look out in that field. What do you see?"

She looks where he told her to look. Darkness has fallen, and the stage blazes like a small sun set down on the field. From the bench seats, there is a buzz of chatter rising from the audience, a hum of anticipation.

"When I got started way back in '73, was a panic on, and everybody was saying *all was lost*. The doom and gloomers had us all licked and laid in our graves. But me and my little show—wasn't nothing to us but a couple of acrobats and a donkey and a puppet back then— me and my little show, we went *all the way* from Indiana to the golden valleys of California playing to a *full house* every single night. And while we was about wasn't nobody jumping off no bridges. Wasn't nobody swinging from a beam in the barn. Wasn't nobody putting no shotgun down his throat. We put a stop to all that when we was in town. You understand what I'm saying, gal? You know what that means?"

He talks so much and so fast that Antoinette is too clumsy, too slow, to catch all of his words as they flow from his tongue. She is trying to get her hands around a splash of water, snatching at it, cupping it before it can get away from her. She frowns, looks out at the show again. Murmurs, "I think so."

"Ha! Damn right you do!" Doc Bell says.

She does. Yes. She couldn't say how, exactly, but she does. Doc Bell's show, shadowy bits and pieces to her before, turns suddenly solid, a thing.

"Lil," Doc Bell calls. He is walking backwards into the field, not exactly turning to shadow—he is too big, too bright, for that— but melding with the night air. "Lil, strike that tent! We're done with Sheba! Tonight this gal's going onstage with me!"

And then he lopes off, leaving Antoinette to watch him open-mouthed as his words ring in her ears. *Onstage with me tonight.* Does he mean her? Onstage, where his people sing and clown and dance all night?

She turns and looks for Lily, as if that will tell her the answer, but Lily's face in the moonlight that has broken through clouds above looks just as bewildered as Antoinette feels. And there are others. Three of Doc Bell's men and as many women stand amidst the cars and trucks, looking at each other, saying nothing, any of them, these normally raucous people, as if Doc Bell has carried off their tongues in his back pocket.

Then someone comes up beside Antoinette from the other direction. The long-faced woman she has seen arm in arm with the seamstress who once mended her hat. The woman has kept her distance whenever she and Antoinette passed in a hall. She stands a few paces back now, her arms crossed, looking down at Antoinette. She clears her throat harshly.

"Mr. Fleet been after me to fetch you for a walk," she says in a wooden voice. "Guess this is good a time to start as any. Come on."

She holds out her hand. Antoinette looks at it. The lights and sounds of the stage, the vision of Doc Bell, all of it swims among her thoughts, churning them, making her head pound, making her unsteady on her feet. What should she do now? She looks off into the dark, to where Sheba's tent should stand, but Lily hasn't lit its torches and without their light, she cannot find it. When she looks again, the woman's hand is still extended to her.

She takes it. The woman guides her by the arm off the road, and they step into the field, toward the stage.

AFTER THAT . . . after that, everything turns inside out all over again.

At the showgrounds, the backstage tent sucks her into a whirlwind of lunging and limbering bodies, of feathers and pants and frocks slipped on and off in an instant, horns and baby dolls and cabbages and umbrellas and coal scuttles and dead chickens passed among quick hands, cackles of laughter, shrieks of pain, hats of every description that seem to fly constantly through the air, coiling ropes of lamp smoke, lassos and cleavers and red balls and red boots and bouquets of red roses and bloody hams and bulging water bottles, grimaces and curses, *'Scuse me*s and *Dangitall*s and *Aw, blow off*s and *Shut your yap*s and even, once Antoinette has ceased shying from them where she sits in

181

a chair in the corner, *Welcome, Mademoiselle*, from a slovenly hulk of a man who takes and tenderly kisses her hand.

And the stage. Not the tiny platform she had seen from the field, flanked by a pair of torches. Now, a room whose dimensions she can't fathom, whose walls she can reach out in every direction and never touch.

Out there in the darkness, in the light-blind darkness that surrounds her, a sea of people spreads out in every direction around her when Doc Bell calls her out from the backstage tent during one of his lectures. But they are not people like those who shuffled, whispering and pointing, through Sheba's tent. *Lookit that! You believe it?* They are not like the doctors and visitors to Dunham Hospital. *Unbelievable! I've never seen anything like it!* No, there is something different that radiates from them as Doc Bell stalks around the stage, gesticulating and bowing, now waving a hand in her direction, now pointing a finger at one person after another in the audience. His voice rises and catches the night wind like a bat and soars and flits as if it will come to rest on every lap, every shoulder, every opened hand before the night is through. They sigh in waves, they gasp in surprise and sympathy, they send up a murmur when Doc Bell pauses that is like a caress on the cheek.

This gal was done for, and it was pitiful to see! A collective moan escapes them. *But Doc Bell don't never give up, no matter how hopeless a body is, no matter what-all them authorities got to say.* They nod and lisp their approval. *Now look here and see what kind of miracle Doc Bell's tonics can make! If* this here gal *can rise up from her deathbed and breathe again, if* this here gal *can rise up and walk again, just look at her, ladies and gentlemen, if* this here gal *can rise up and live again, just think what a little of the same tonic can do for you! Come on out here, gal! Throw down that cane! Come on!* He drops his arms, and steps back, back, back, and Antoinette feels something rising from the audience, flowing from them, pouring onto the stage. A few of them will even cry, but not from pain or sadness, the only cause of tears she has ever known.

And then Doc Bell's people rush out from everywhere at once and fan out into the audience, sacks and crates of Doc Bell's tonics and balms slung from their shoulders. A crowd rushes forward, pushes and shoves to reach them, howls and cries to get their attention, waves open hands and fists clenched with bills and coins to attract them. Doc Bell's people. They become part of him, extra arms and legs. And the crowd devours them.

One holds back to lead Antoinette off the stage and back into the tent behind it. Her escort takes her arm, or places a hand on her shoulder, or even grasps her hand, as little Pete, the acrobat, does now. He is small as a child, barely high as Antoinette's shoulder, and she feels almost as if she ought to be caring for him. He pats her hand as they walk, as the little spangles in his black shirt and tights catch the torchlight, and a shine dances across the incongruous bald spot on the top of his head. "There, now, easy, easy, that's it, that's it," he says. "That's a girl, that's a girl. Hold on. Watch the step, watch the step." Once safely inside, he looks up, gives her a gummy grin, and lets go. On other nights, it might be others whose names she has learned: Kidwell, the sloppy man who first welcomed her; Tildy, the woman who now fetches her for a walk along the road every morning; even Mr. Fleet, who grinned that first night and assured her, "Look at you out there, gal! You're a natural!"

Later, lying in her boardinghouse bed, Antoinette feels she will never again sleep, but the wakefulness is not unpleasant, and when morning comes, quickly, she finds she has slept deeply. She opens her eyes. Afternoon arrives and goes. The day wanes, the shadows lengthen, the air cools.

And once more, the show begins.

SHE CONTINUES to eat her breakfast alone in her room, as Felix Conger told her she must. But now, one of the others brings her plate up to her. And knocks. And hands it to her, with a napkin, and asks if she would like a glass of water. Often it is Tildy, who asks after her sleep and reports on the weather they'll meet when they step outside later. Sometimes it is Mr. Fleet. Once, even, Mr. Fleet's wife, who scowled but kept her tongue other than to say, "It ain't hot, but it ain't no better when it is nohow."

Tildy usually came much earlier, before breakfast, when it was barely light, "before the day get full of people," she said. She waited while Antoinette gathered her hat and her cane, and then they made their way out the front door, arm in arm, and down the front walk, and out into the road, where a stray horse and wagon with a lone driver or the occasional meandering mule and junk cart might pass them, but usually, they had the stripped fields to themselves. Most often, neither talked, and the only sound to accompany their footsteps was the lowing of distant cows or the cawing of crows passing overhead. Sometimes, a bit of conversation passed between them, like a bubble that rose out of the water and then burst.

"I wish them mice in the walls be quiet at night," Tildy might say.

Or, "I can't seem to find my good stockings."

Or, "Mr. Fleet looking a bit peaked these days."

Or, "Salem Locks. I never heard of no place with a name like that."

At first Antoinette just listened. Then, after a while, she would offer an equally brief reply, like "Maybe they got under the bed."

"Could be," Tildy would say. "I'll take a look there."

Tildy's grasp was steady, her pace as regular as the ticking of a clock. When they moved on to a new town, she pointed out what there was to see to Antoinette: "There go that pumpkin they said got too big to pick." "This is the beech tree that whistle like a bird when the wind get high." They would stop, and look, and rest in the meantime, and move on.

One morning, Antoinette decides to ask a question. "Where is that man Felix Conger?"

Tildy chuckles dryly. "Run off a while ago. And good riddance, too."

Encouraged, Antoinette tries another. "And...Sauer?"

Tildy looks at her with a cocked eyebrow. "Been a long time since I seen that one, now that you mention it." She shrugs her shoulders. "Don't know."

"And the lady that sews?" Antoinette has not seen her alone or with Tildy in the boardinghouse halls or on the showgrounds for weeks. It is as if she has blown away.

Tildy's step slows, and Antoinette thinks at first that she has said something improper, that Tildy is not going to answer. They walk in silence. Then Tildy says, "You got a butterfly in a jar, you can't keep it in there long. Either it's going to die, or you got to open the jar."

Pretty things, Antoinette thinks Tildy is talking about. She pulls her shawl tighter around her shoulders and tries to calm the throbbing behind her eyes. For the rest of the way, past a muddy cow pond and a field where a few brown horses graze and toss their tails, they stay silent. But after that they fall back into conversation, bits and snatches about other things. What it is like to swallow a sword. All the cooking and cleaning and feeding and sewing Tildy did before Doc Bell's show. The Dunham Hospital for Incurable Children. How much there is to Pennsylvania, a state that seems to go on without end.

A FEW DAYS later, the knock at Antoinette's door comes early, just after sunrise. She waits, as the door opens, for Tildy to step inside.

But it is not Tildy who enters. It is, instead, a man in a dark gray homburg and matching coat, pressed black trousers, shoes that look new. Antoinette stares at the shoes for a moment, then runs her eyes back up to the face, the eyes that gaze back into her own.

Sauer?

That he might return, after so long, she had never imagined. She stares openly, as if her eyes might be playing tricks on her. A thousand questions fly through her mind. Why did he just disappear like that? Where did he go? And how did he manage to find Bell's show again?

He takes off his hat, comes forward, picks up the lone chair and sets it in front of her where she sits on the bed. Sits down himself. Just as he has done so many times before. A crow caws outside the window, and the shadow of its flapping wings plays quickly across the bare wood floor. It is just after sunup, and birds are flocking in the trees, as they do every morning. How easily, how quickly, she could fall back into their old routine.

He looks down at his hands and clears his throat. Watching his fingers, the hat, she is troubled again by a sudden suspicion. This is not Sauer. Not the doctor who stumbled into her room, bleary-eyed and musty, unshaved, his shirt unstarched, on all those mornings she remembers. This is someone else.

He interrupts her thoughts by speaking, finally. "I came to Bell's show last night. I sat in the audience through the whole thing."

She watches him warily.

"I saw what Bell is doing to you."

His face reddens, and he looks away, out the window, his arms folded across his chest. Finally he shakes his head.

"Well, there will be no more of that now," he says gruffly.

She takes him in once more, his impatience, his traveling clothes. This is the man who left her behind. Who left them all behind. Who has found for himself, clearly, better things.

"No more what?" she says. "No more of me having someplace warm to sleep at night?"

Sauer frowns, looks confused. "No, that is not what I meant."

"No more of me getting enough to eat? No more people coming around to see if, if I'm, if I—" She is wheezing now, her chest tight, and a fit of coughing seizes her.

When it passes and she looks at him again, he is floating in the midst of a thousand blinking lights, yellow, white, blue, pinpoints, small suns. She hears him shift, scrape the chair legs against the floor before he settles himself again.

He leans toward her and waves a hand as if he can clear the air. "Listen. I have found a position. At a poor hospital in Pittsburgh. It is not much, it pays very little, but enough. And they will...take you. I have arranged it for you. You will have a room, food, real medicine. You will have everything you need."

The chattering of the birds rises, surrounds them, blends with the blinking lights as if giving the lights voice. Gradually the lights thin out, grow fewer, dimmer, until they are gone and she can see clearly the man seated in front of her.

He is not that Sauer anymore. Was he ever? She had looked upon him as a last remnant of Dunham Hospital, its white-coated doctors, its starched nurses, their careful needles, thermometers, spoons full of castor oil. But if they were careful of her, those doctors and nurses, why had they turned her out in the cold, just as Felix Conger said? She'd taken comfort in Sauer's probing and testing, his inquiry into her well-being. But if that was what Sauer had been doing, why, then, had he come back only now, like this? As if she would be here waiting forever? As if he might change his mind again in a week, in a month, and forget about her once more?

"No," she says.

Sauer blinks, looks confused. "No?" he echoes. "You do not wish to go to—?"

"No," she says again, louder.

Sauer opens his mouth to say something, then closes it and bows his head. For some moments he stays that way. He finally says, "Miss Riddick."

He has never called her by name before. He fingers the brim of his hat in his lap. "We have passed many mornings here," he says.

"That's over with." She is surprised to hear herself say it.

He doesn't argue. The light around them shifts from the wan glow of early morning to the stark sunlight of another day, pressing into corners, showing the ridges and knobs of her hands in her lap.

"My wife, Greta," Sauer says slowly, haltingly. "We were not young when we married. I never expected to marry at all, not as I was then, but..." He pauses, collects his thoughts. "Greta would read to me in the evening, after I came in from seeing patients all day, through dinner many times. She waited for me. She would have me sit in the parlor next to her, and she would read to me her favorites. Bryant and Whittier. And Longfellow. Forests and streams, storms and sunrises. In a clear voice, for an hour or more, she read to me. She was raised among such good men, you see. In those few rooms we had let, with barely enough heat in winter, she invited them in with us as I would never have thought to do."

He stops there and fingers his hat again. "After she died, for a long time, I thought it was best that I put Greta and our life out of my mind. But I was wrong."

Antoinette stares at him, puzzled. What has any of it to do with her, people she doesn't know, this dead wife he has never before spoken of? She looks around the room. "This is not your parlor," she reminds him.

He nods, stands up, smoothes his trousers, and takes something from his pocket.

"I invite you to call on me, Miss Riddick," he says, "whenever you wish to. Here is where you may find me." In her lap, he lays a small, brown book no thicker than her little finger. Then he pats his empty pocket, walks to the door and leaves.

Once again, he is gone.

It is some moments before she picks the thing up. It's bound in faded, well-fingered leather that has tattered where it bends, like the worn-out schoolbooks she used long ago as a child. She could throw it out, and with it, all traces of him and his foolish invitation, made as if she might just come visit him for afternoon tea on a whim. But she runs her fingers along the lettering on the cover, which is no more than a faint indentation now, looping letters that spell out *On the Occasion of a Visit to Harper's Wood*. For a long time, she does nothing with it. Then she opens it. On the right-hand page is the silhouette of a bare tree with a broad canopy, no words at all. On the left, over the faint design in the endpaper, are written Sauer's name and the address of a hospital in Pittsburgh.

When she finally stands, even leaning hard on her cane, she can barely make her hips move. She sighs, nevertheless, and paces slowly around the room, restless, unsettled by Sauer's visit. She wishes Tildy would hurry. Lately her punctuality has been slipping, and she has come late in the morning sometimes, or not at all. Antoinette goes to the dresser to fetch her hat. Perhaps she will not wait this morning. Perhaps she will go and fetch Tildy today.

A FEW DAYS later, when the show is outside a town Tildy has told Antoinette is called Harrellsburg, Doc Bell does all three of his lectures without calling her out onto the stage.

The next night, it happens again.

"Don't mean a thing," Mr. Fleet comes over and tells her as she sits in her corner, watching Doc Bell's people carom around her, changing costumes and readying themselves to go onstage. "Lineup get switched around all the time. Doc Bell like to keep folks guessing. He bring you out again soon."

As the third night stretches on, Doc Bell's people seem smaller, dimmer, farther away the more she tries to see them clearly. Antoinette blinks, wondering whether something is happening now to her eyesight. But they sound muffled, too, almost as if they are whispering, trying not to let her hear what they say.

Back at the boardinghouse, she drags herself to her room in the back, another out-of-the-way spot that is around a corner and down a short hall devoid of other rooms, even a rug. In her room, all she can hear is the wind and the crickets outside the black window, as if she is alone in the ramshackle building. When she lights a candle, shadows jump up along the walls, cast by the chair beside the bed, the deep corners, the mirror placed on top of the chest of drawers.

It is so cold she thinks to sleep in the red frock, but it must be washed, so she unbuttons it and drops it from her shoulders. What has been nagging at the back of her mind, in the quiet, suddenly takes shape. Maybe Doc Bell sent the seamstress away. Maybe he got rid of Felix Conger, too. Maybe, despite all his talk about sticking with his people, there were a few he didn't keep. She puts her frock in the basin on the chest of drawers and reaches for the pitcher of water beside it, but the reflection of the candle flame draws her eye to the mirror leaning against the wall and stops her hand in mid-gesture.

In the glass, around the flame, she sees not the self she expects but dark bits of something else. A hip bulge, like a cluster of rocks in a sack. Hands shriveled to birdsfoot claws. A chest tight-fisted as dried apples. And a big, dented loaf of forehead pushed so low that it barely leaves room for the eyes that stare back at her.

This is what people came to see in Sheba's tent. And this was what drew the stares of visitors at Dunham Hospital. Not a miracle. This. No wonder their eyes widened and they turned away from her. No wonder nobody came to visit her bedside, to hold her hand and to cry over her, as they did for the others. To take her home.

She leaves the pitcher untouched, the frock unwashed, and curls herself in the lumpy bed, listening to the cricketsong until she falls into an exhausted, restless sleep.

THE NEXT MORNING, she awakens so late there is full sunshine streaming in through the curtainless window. Nobody has brought her breakfast. Antoinette lies motionless. Perhaps she will stay in bed. But the thought of Lily rapping at her door moves her to lever herself up to sitting. Pinpoints of light flash around her. She gets up and dresses.

Out in the hall, she makes her way around the corner and to the door of Tildy's room, but there is no answer when she knocks. The dining room is empty, neither the owner nor anyone else about. There are faint sounds from some of the other rooms, but Tildy would not be visiting, Antoinette believes. So she wraps herself in her shawl and goes outside.

The wind has died down, and the sun has warmed the day to an almost springlike feel. But there is nobody outside, either. A few auburn and black chickens strut and peck around the back of the house, near a well, and birds flit overhead. But nothing else stirs in the field of tall grass that rolls out toward squares of distant pasture turned over for the winter's long sleep.

Tildy has given up walking with her. That must be it. Antoinette considers this idea for a long moment during which she stands still, seeing nothing in front of her, hearing nothing around her. Then she grips her cane and walks around to the back of the chicken coop, where she calls Tildy's name.

Down a short slope lies a small pond. A white goose stands on the edge. In the water floats a piece of cloth that, as Antoinette draws near, bulges with pockets of trapped air. It is a gray and black plaid flannel, a pattern Antoinette knows.

It is Tildy's frock.

Tildy drifts motionless, only her back and shoulders and the back of her head above the black water. Even with her cane, Antoinette nearly falls getting down to the water's edge. The goose hops up and flaps away. Antoinette looks around her, sees no hope of help, and steps into the pond.

The cold bite of water around her ankles makes her gasp, and the bottom slides and sinks beneath her, as if it will swallow her. She stops, then takes another step. The grip of the cold rising up her legs makes her wheeze, but she keeps going. Deeper in, and she sees that the pond is a larger, wider expanse than she realized, that Tildy is only a small clump of floating leaves, far away. The water has risen above her waist before Antoinette stops again, her chest heaving for air as if it is her face underwater, as if the floating green scum and fetid smell are closing over her head. She reaches out with the handle of her cane, but it slips off Tildy's shoulder uselessly, and the sight of that almost makes her collapse. The water is a stone-hard wall pressing in around her ribs now. But the next time she reaches out, the handle of her cane hooks Tildy's collar.

The hardest part is at the end, with Tildy near the edge, no longer supported by the water. Antoinette can barely drag the weight of her halfway into the muddy cattails, where she collapses with her arms around Tildy, shaking so violently that she cannot breathe or make any sound at all.

But she doesn't need to. Tildy sputters water and gags and coughs. Then she grunts and cries out and pries at Antoinette's hands until she loosens the grip around her middle.

THE NEXT THING she hears is laughter. Voices in the hall outside her door as she lies in her bed, where she has awakened to the bright, pale hue of a late autumn morning. And conversation. Someone says her name, and she slips back into sleep.

The comedian, Mr. Kidwell, is sitting beside her bed when she next awakens, wearing a black coat and bow tie that Antoinette has seen him don before going onstage. He stands up, bows so deeply toward her that he staggers a little, lifts her hand in his own damp one and kisses it. "Well done, my dear," he says in a deep voice, without a trace of a smile on his stubbly face.

"Tildy..." is all Antoinette can manage.

"Will no doubt be singing your praises as soon as her bruises heal," Mr. Kidwell replies, and winks.

Sometime after that, she opens her eyes again and finds Mr. Fleet nodding beside her, a pipe about to drop from his lower lip. When he hears her move, he sits up and takes the pipe in his hand.

"You got everybody talking, gal," he says. "Hell, even Louise won't shut up about it. Boy offa some farm out there saw the whole thing. Said ain't nobody can't swim ever go in there, nor most that can, neither. Said a man drownt in there before the war, and he wouldn't a jumped in for his own mama!"

He smiles at her. "Doc Bell got a tough act to follow tonight, now don't he, gal?"

There's a rap at the door, and Mr. Fleet turns around and yells, "Let the gal rest! Come back later!" Then he picks up a glass of milk from the floor and asks if Antoinette is hungry.

The next time she wakes, it is night again. Quiet. She wonders whether she has been dreaming, but she sees the half-empty glass of milk on the chair where Mr. Fleet left it for her. The cricketsong rises and falls melodically now, a lullaby on which she drifts, remembering. Who was crowding outside her door, chattering? What will they say to her the next day? She tests her arms and legs, feels the strength coming back to them after the draining cold of the awful pond, the fright of seeing Tildy like that. Now she will have visitors. She knows the voices she heard in the hall, excited, happy, talking about her.

Maybe even Doc Bell himself, who never comes to the board-inghouses, will come to her room to see her. She wonders how he will bring her back onstage, what surprise he will have for her, how he will use this new story about her that is on everyone's lips.

Later, she hears a stirring and opens her eyes to a room filled with a strange light, nearly green, as if a moth has spread the dust from its wings throughout the air. The fluttering of birds in the eaves announces that it is morning. Antoinette rubs her eyes and looks around, but nothing is familiar, as if she has left her room for another while she slept, or the furnishings have melted and merged with the air, creating broad impressions where there were once firm objects. Near the door there is a movement, and she looks that way at a shape so tall it scrapes the ceiling, and it comes toward her, bending low toward her where she lies in her bed.

"You awake again. I got some broth for you."

Tildy, her long shadow on the wall behind her, leans her face down close to Antoinette's.

It is so good to see her that Antoinette forgets all about Doc Bell. She takes in Tildy's steady brown eyes, the bowl in her hands, the white strips wrapped firmly around her ribcage.

"That's some grip you got," she says, holding out a spoon she blows on.

Antoinette swallows and only then realizes she is very hungry. After she has drunk half of what Tildy brought her, she looks at the bandages again.

Tildy looks down, pats herself gingerly, and says, "I'll heal up fine, they say."

Antoinette tries to speak, but only a croak comes out.

"You just take it easy," Tildy says. "I be right here, you need anything. See that?" She looks behind herself, but Antoinette can't see what she glances at. "Made me a bedroll so I can sleep in here with you, case you need anything."

Out in the hall, it is again quiet, Antoinette notices. No voices, no footfalls.

"Did Doc Bell come?" she finally gets out.

Tildy thinks for a while before she says anything. Eventually she says, "They all took off this morning. Mr. Fleet said the show was going to Grangerville. 'Bout a day from here." She reaches out, pulls the blanket up to Antoinette's chin and leans over her, her face graver than usual, almost angry. "Told me Doc Bell said soon as you well, he be happy to have Sheba back in her tent."

Antoinette thinks Tildy must be wrong. Sheba's tent? Doc Bell couldn't have said that. Not now. But Tildy is looking at her intently and says, "No need to worry about it right now. You ain't fit to travel yet. You get some sleep."

Antoinette closes her eyes. Wills herself to sleep again. But she is rested now, the day is upon her, and sleep refuses to come.

THE BOY WHO watched Antoinette pull Tildy out of the pond is the one who drives them. A gangly white lad with freckles and mud-caked overalls who smells of barn stalls and surprises them by carrying all of Tildy's bags and her prop trunk and Antoinette's satchel out the front door in one load.

It's been two weeks now, and Tildy can move about without wincing. Antoinette can sit up and walk around her room a bit without exhausting herself. After Tildy has settled up with the boardinghouse owner, the two of them stand in the road out front as the boy, whose name is Wilbur Foats, straps their belongings to the rear of the topless, ancient Pope-Hartford touring sedan he says he has been allowed to take for half a day. It looks more like a pile of castoff tin and pipes than a car, but Wilbur Foats has given assurances about its reliability.

Once they are on the road, Tildy's worries about the wind taking Antoinette's hat evaporate. Wilbur Foats squeezes nothing more than the speed of an exhausted farm horse from the car, and the countryside around them barely seems to move at all. The roar it makes is terrific. Periodically, birds bullet out of the trees along the road to escape the approaching racket.

After a while Antoinette thinks of the luggage behind them and imagines what it will be like when they take out all that Tildy has packed. She still sees the frocks, pink and blue ones, white and yellow ones, dresses so beautiful that it was hard to believe, looking at them, that there was no body inside of them. We'll start with the ribbons, Tildy had said as they folded and packed them. The buttons next. The hooks and eyes. Some even had lace, which you had to be very, very careful with or it would tear apart in your fingers. Once they had reclaimed the easy parts, they would take a ripper to the seams and begin the delicate work of disassembling skirts and bodices, sleeves and collars. It would take a while. But they would have enough fabric and notions to make much of what they were going to need at first.

At this pace, it will take them better than an hour to reach Portins Mill. They've bought some leftover chicken and corn and apple cider from the boardinghouse owner to take with them for later. They will eat it off of a dusty counter in a boarded-up shop off of Main Street, one that Wilbur Foats tells them has been sitting vacant for so many years the owner has stopped running advertisements for it.

And though Antoinette finds it strange at first to travel without the others, to head where Doc Bell and his people are not going, the strangeness does not last for long. There is too much new to think about. Tildy sitting straight beside her, her face turned toward the brown fields and whatever thoughts lie out there for her, but her arm linked with Antoinette's. The town of Portins Mill, which Wilbur Foats says is not much but some big, shady houses and a general store and a church and a fountain and boys who would take your best cat's eye or oxblood if you were foolish enough to shoot marbles with them. The necessity of learning to sew, if she is going to help Tildy with the dressmaking, which she has agreed to do to convince Tildy to even attempt the journey they have embarked on.

After a while the bouncing, swaying ride itself is enough to tire her and bring back the pain that had left her for the whole of the morning. Tildy looks her way, frowns, and pats the soft expanse of her own lap. Antoinette mouths *No* at first, but Tildy insists until she takes off her hat and, with Tildy's help, lowers herself and rests her head there. The tension goes out of her shoulders and back and hips, and she breathes a long sigh that is swallowed up in the straining sound of the motorcar's old engine. Tildy's hand falls across Antoinette's shoulder and rests there lightly. And Antoinette closes her eyes, finds that she can summon a lost memory: of warm breath on her ear and cheek, of the slow rumble of a heart close to her own. Of a voice low like hers saying *I don't want to let you go, but I have to*. Of hands that held her tightly, for one last time, before Antoinette relinquished herself to the inevitable tug of sleep.

Thread

Matilda "Tildy" South

———

I NEVER called her nothing but Miss Antoinette. She said call her Antoinette, but that never did feel right to me. So she was Miss Antoinette to me, from the day we left Doc Bell's show right up until the end.

We got us a little storefront in Portins Mill with some rooms in the back. Place was on a side street a ways off Main and not a lot of people about. There was big elm trees all along the street, so it was always nice and cool and quiet. More than a few days I spent sitting by the front window just staring out at the street. The shop wasn't much to look at. The sign over the door still said H.E. SMILEY & SONS LOCK-SMITHS and the floor and the walls and even the little counter in the back all had holes from the machines that used to be bolted there. You could still smell all that oil and metal in the air. And it was dust enough to make it look like it was a hundred years since Mr. Smiley closed up.

When I took Miss Antoinette her soup at midday, she said did I put up a new sign yet. She was still resting herself all day then. I said,

Well, I guess I can do that. I took Mr. Smiley down and did up something simple for the front window that said MATILDA SOUTH SEAMSTRESS.

WHEN THEM dressmaker's forms come from the Sears & Roebuck they did look a little lonely with nary a frock to cover them up. So I took out two of them frocks Marie left behind that I didn't rip up and set them out. Had to pin up the skirts to keep them out of the dust, but that didn't bother them none. I walked over to the general store and got a broom and a dustpan and a bucket and some soap, but I couldn't never seem to get around to using them on all that old dust and grit and oil. I just kept looking at them frocks shining in yellow and cream and pink and thinking wasn't no way I was ever going to get them old floors and shelves looking that clean and perfect.

One day when the elm trees was finally bare Miss Antoinette said why don't you stay and eat your soup with me. I said I guess so. I wasn't really eating no midday soup then nor much of anything else. But I didn't want Miss Antoinette to be lonely or think I was still afraid of her like I used to be, so I did it. She asked me about the shop every day and who was coming in and what was they wanting. I told her all about how I was planning this and that and the other. Finally she said she was feeling good enough to come out and see it all tomorrow.

I was up all night dusting and sweeping and scrubbing. You shoulda seen the filth I poured out of there, one bucket at a time. It's a wonder I didn't kill every leaf of grass in the yard out back. Miss Antoinette come out in that big black hat of hers and said it looked like my plans was coming right along.

FIRST WHITE lady come in the next day blushing a little and looking for a hat for her daughter's wedding in three weeks. I make dresses, I said. I don't do hats. You need blocks and glues and such for that. I could tell from how big her eyes got she was used to people doing what she said. She said she had a tailor picked out in Boston to make the dress and wouldn't think of using the likes of me for fine work such as that. Can I at least do up some little flower baskets for the table settings? And decorate the gazebo with ribbons and bunting? And on and on. I said she sure had a lot to do in a hurry and I was sorry I couldn't help her.

It wasn't long before Miss Antoinette was well enough to sit up and learn some easy stitches. And a good thing, too. That lady came back two weeks later for the wedding gown when that tailor in Boston didn't work out.

I GET THE *Variety* every month now. It do bring back memories to read about them vaudeville shows and such. I expect one day I will see Marie in there and find out she found herself another show somewhere, though she hardly need one. The *Variety* said that Doc Bell's Miracles and Mirth Medicine Show played in a little theater in New York City for a while, but it closed up pretty fast. Then Doc Bell joined up with a carnival that was out in Wichita at the time. Haven't seen word one about him or the rest of them since.

My Eloise been with me almost five years now, and she still say to me, Tildy, when you going to forget about all that playacting nonsense and hang up your dancing shoes for good? Her people being from around here, she don't think much past Portins Mill in her mind. That ain't to say she is a woman of small heart, because she ain't so at all. But I take the Philadelphia paper once a week and the *Collier's*, too. My traveling days are over, I tell her, but it still don't hurt to know a little bit about the rest of the world.

WAS MARIE that said to me Miss Antoinette had sides to her didn't nobody know about, and though I come to see Marie was wrong about a lot of things, she was right sometimes. Miss Antoinette got the hang of sewing pretty quick and she even took to doing some of the embroidery work, which never was my favorite thing to do. Then, when we was between orders, she started to sew the strangest things out of scraps, shapes you never did see or even think of before, and who knew what to do with them? I put them in a basket on a stool next to the front window, and white ladies coming in started to pick them out and say, What is this? Is it a face? Is it a flower? And I said back, I don't know, and they looked at me funny and sniffed and put it back exactly where they got it. After a time, I set the basket right up front on the counter with the coinbox.

Children never did ask such questions when they come in with their mamas. Little girls just picked one up and put it up against their cheek or their stomach or their knee and said, Mama, can I have one? And before their mamas could say anything back, I said, Just take it. It belong to you, now.

WE WAS GOING to put in some flowers out back, but by the time spring come, we was so busy with orders I forgot. But I told Miss Antoinette it was time she come out in the shop where we got all the needles and threads and scissors handy. No need for her to sit in her room all day by herself.

She said no, thank you, she prefer to be out back in the garden.

That was a funny thing to say. Wasn't nothing out there but a big, gnarly willow tree and a little bit of grass. Back of that was a cornfield stretched out far as you could see. Soon as it was warm, we took a chair and a table out there and set everything up for her. You sure this is how you want it, I said to her. She just settled herself down in that black hat of hers and said, Yes, this is fine.

Seemed damp to me, but I left her there. And she was there every day it didn't rain. Got so things was regular in the shop, deliveries and orders, keeping the books and cutting the patterns, and we even got us a nice black Singer machine after a while, fancy model that could just about put stitches through wood if you wanted it to. People was coming to me saying, Matilda, can you sew me the sheets and blankets and a nice little skirt with plenty of lace for the bassinette? Matilda, can you make me some doilies that look like my blue hydrangeas for the parlor? I was glad for all the business, but was up to me to say yes or no, and I never did forget that. One day in the middle of the day, I got up after one of them ladies went bustling out the door and put up the sign that said CLOSED.

Then I took my work out back and sat with Miss Antoinette a while. We got to talking easy about this and that and other things. I told her about Marie and her husband and how he come to take her home one time and how she must of decided to go. Miss Antoinette told me all about Dunham Hospital for Incurable Children and how they sent her away when she got to be too much trouble. What kind of hospital do a thing like that when people come there because of trouble in the first place, I wanted to know. She said that's just how she see it, too.

Wasn't but the middle of May, but the day got to be finer than any one I remember. Air so warm and light it felt like a cotton ball against your cheek. Sky so blue you want to just reach up your arms and grab a bunch of it. Everything bursting green and fresh and even the old willow dropping little green twirls of leaves that float down and down till they light on your skirt or lap or shoe. The wind just picked up and blew and blew and sprinkled all those little green leaves on us till it seemed like something silly you wished for when you was a little child and then forgot about it and now it was happening.

Miss Antoinette said, Tildy, promise me you won't do a thing like that again.

I was going to say back, Like what?, but then I knew what she was talking about. It was the one time we ever spoke of it. She was holding a needle in those long, fine fingers of hers and looking at me out from under the shadow of her hat.

Sometimes I think back and think she must have knew Eloise was coming to me. But I guess I seen enough of Madame Svetlana's tricks and Doc Bell's nonsense to know that nobody can know that. More likely, I guess, she must have knew Eloise might be coming to me, and I better be ready.

☙ ❧

IT WAS A little more than a year and a half that Miss Antoinette was with me before she couldn't work no more. When it pained her too much to walk or even sit up, she took to her bed. You just need some rest, I said to her. You just lay easy, I will take care of all the orders myself.

And I did, for a month, but she wasn't getting no better and she asked me one morning to fetch Dr. Sauer.

I thought her mind was finally giving out on her and she forgot where she was now, so I sent for Dr. Fitch, who everybody said was a good man and took Negro patients. He come the next day and went in her room for almost a hour. Then about a week later, when it was raining so hard it was chopping little branches off the elm trees and filling up the street with them, I looked up from the counter and there was Dr. Sauer.

His brown coat was dripping wet and he hadn't any hat on his head, so I dried him up as best I could and sat him down. He asked me how I was doing and I said fine and I asked him the same thing, and he said he had a wife now and a daughter in Pittsburgh.

Then he asked me where she is, and I pointed to the door that leads to the back where we got our rooms. He stood there just looking at the door a good long time. The rain got gentle and quiet, so as to make every breath and every footfall loud on the ear. Dr. Sauer sighed and said thank you, Miss South, and walked over there.

"Wait," I said. "You forgot your doctor bag."

It was sitting right there on the counter where he left it, next to the coinbox and the spools of lace and ribbon.

He looked at it a minute and smiled and shook his head, no.

Then he went in. Through the door, I could hear him walk down the hall and knock and go in. I could hear the chair squeak when he sat down, and his voice saying something, and hers saying something back, but I couldn't tell what they said.

A little while later, not long after the rain stopped, he come back out front to tell me she was gone.

Acknowledgments

This work would not have come to be without the help of many. Grants from the National Endowment for the Arts, the Maryland State Arts Council, and the Prince George's County Arts and Humanities Council made it possible for me to conduct research and devote time to writing; I am most grateful for the support. Many of these stories were born during residencies at the Mary Anderson Center for the Arts; I am indebted to the staff and patrons who gave me the gift of time there. I thank the patient readers who offered me invaluable advice and encouragement over the years about the many parts and versions of the manuscript: Donna Hemans, Doreen Baingana, Angela Threatt, Karen Outen, Kaija Blalock, Michael Martone, my fellow workshop participants at the Vermont Postgraduate Writers' Conference, and my husband, Kurt Keefner. And finally, tremendous thanks to Rosalie Morales Kearns for the amazing work she does through Shade Mountain Press and for making this book a reality.

In the course of doing research for this book, I consulted a wide variety of resources to help me understand forms of popular entertainment of the early twentieth century and the lives of people of that era. Among the most important were *Step Right Up*, by Brooks McNamara; *Snake Oil, Hustlers and Hambones: The American Medicine*

Show, by Ann Anderson; *The Fabulous Kelley: He Was King of the Medicine Men*, by Thomas P. Kelley, Jr.; *No Time for Tears*, by Katheryn M. Patterson; *Flu: The Story of the Great Influenza Pandemic of 1918 and the Search for the Virus That Caused It*, by Gina Kolata; *Good for What Ails You: Music of the Medicine Shows, 1926–1937* (two CDs); photograph collections of the Library of Congress, the Schomburg Center for Research in Black Culture, and the historical societies of Fulton and Lancaster Counties; and the collection of the now-defunct Dime Museum of Baltimore.

Also from Shade Mountain Press

NOVELS

Kirsten Imani Kasai, *The House of Erzulie*

A tale of obsession and racial guilt on an 1850s Louisiana plantation. Editors' Choice, *Historical Novels Review*. "Skillfully blends an atmosphere of hallucinatory tension with well-researched explorations into 19th-century beliefs"—*Library Journal*.

Vanessa Garcia, *White Light*

A young Cuban-American artist distills her grief, rage, and love onto the canvas. Praised by Nobel laureate Wole Soyinka for its "lyrical pace and texture." An NPR Best Book of 2015. First prize, International Latino Book Award.

Yi Shun Lai, *Not a Self-Help Book: The Misadventures of Marty Wu*

Marty Wu, compulsive reader of advice manuals, ricochets between a stressful job in New York and the warmth of extended family in Taiwan. Semi-finalist, 2017 Thurber Prize for American Humor.

Lynn Kanter, *Her Own Vietnam*

Decades after serving as a U.S. Army nurse in Vietnam, a woman confronts buried wartime memories and unresolved family issues. Silver Award, Indiefab Book of the Year.

SHORT STORIES

Robin Parks, *Egg Heaven*

Lyrical tales of diner waitresses and their customers, living the un-glamorous life in Southern California. Hailed by *Kenyon Review* as a "welcome addition" to working-class fiction.

The Female Complaint: Tales of Unruly Women, **edited by Rosalie Morales Kearns**

Short story anthology featuring nonconformists, troublemakers, and other indomitable women. Finalist, Indiefab Book of the Year.

POETRY

Mary A. Hood, *All the Spectral Fractures*

New and collected poems by the microbiologist/naturalist/poet. "Spans a prolific career bridging the scientific with the lyric"—Jill McCabe Johnson.

All books are available at our website,
www.ShadeMountainPress.com,
as well as bookstores and online retailers.